THE CAT POSSESSED

Also by Louise Carson

Novels
In Which: Book One of The Chronicles of Deasil Widdy
Measured: Book Two of The Chronicles of Deasil Widdy
The Cat Among Us
The Cat Vanishes
The Cat Between
Executor

Novellas
Mermaid Road

Poetry
A Clearing
Rope: A Tale Told in Prose and Verse
Dog Poems

THE CAT POSSESSED

A MAPLES MYSTERY

LOUISE CARSON

DOUG WHITEWAY, EDITOR

EDITIONS

© 2020, Louise Carson

Cover design by Doowah Design.
Cover icons courtesy of Noun Project.

This book was printed on Ancient Forest Friendly paper.
Printed and bound in Canada by Marquis Book Printing Inc.

We acknowledge the support of the Canada Council for the Arts and the Manitoba Arts Council for our publishing program.

Library and Archives Canada Cataloguing in Publication

Title: The cat possessed : a maples mystery / Louise Carson ; Doug Whiteway, editor.
Names: Carson, Louise, 1957- author.
Identifiers: Canadiana (print) 20200318853 | Canadiana (ebook) 2020031890X | ISBN 9781773240749
  (softcover) | ISBN 9781773240756 (HTML)
Classification: LCC PS8605.A7775 C38 2020 | DDC C813/.6—dc23

Signature Editions
P.O. Box 206, RPO Corydon, Winnipeg, Manitoba, R3M 3S7
www.signature-editions.com

for all my ghosts,
and yours

CONTENTS

PART 1

VIGIL

Kitten was hunting by the light of a nearly full moon. In the semi-darkness in the house, her white legs were a disadvantage, so she crouched, folding them under her black body, became one more shadow in the shadowy living room. Her dilated pupils were as dark as her dark fur; only the pale gold rings around them shone. She waited for the sound of mice.

The other cats were mostly asleep on chairs around the dining room table or upstairs in the bedrooms. Older than she, they usually replied to her demands for midnight games with a yawn or, if she was persistent, a slap. She missed her brothers and sisters, removed from the house one by one.

She missed the banana box in front of the fire where they all used to live. Mother, the big marmalade cat who'd fostered them, still protected Kitten and cosseted her when she was in the mood to be cosseted. Right now, however, she was in the mood for savagery.

She heard a clank from the kitchen and silently ran there. She crouched for a moment, zeroed in on the sound and prepared. She leapt at one cupboard door, nosed it open and entered.

The mouse slithered down a hole surrounding the sink's drainpipe. Kitten sniffed around. Disappointing. She mounted guard by the hole and dozed.

Voices awoke her. She stretched and left the cupboard.

The smoky essence of a tall thin woman hovered over an open drawer. "Now where did I put those stories?" she asked, looking at Kitten. "Do you know?"

Kitten watched as the woman's hand fluttered over a collection of papers.

A different woman's voice called from the living room. It sounded peevish. "I don't know why you think you need them. I need my rest, you know!" Kitten investigated.

Loosely filling one of the rocking chairs with her small misty form, another, older woman rocked impatiently. The first woman floated into the room. "She must have moved them. They're not where I left them." Kitten sat on the hearth rug.

"Well, you've looked for them long enough. I haven't got all night, you know."

"Yes, Mother. Coming, Mother," the tall one said resignedly and made a face at Kitten.

Kitten knew about mothers and their demands: that one hold still to be groomed; that one not shred rugs or upholstery, no matter how delightful the sensation. She blinked twice at the tall woman, in sympathy.

The rocking one continued peevishly. "And these rocking chairs; they've been moved too." Then she noticed the cat, sharpening its claws on the sofa that had displaced the chairs. "This isn't one of yours, is it?"

The tall woman smiled at Kitten. "Gerry must be continuing the good work. Isn't she sweet?" Kitten preened.

The small woman went first, bending low until her head was on the level of the fireplace, then disappearing up the chimney. The other wiggled her fingers at Kitten before following her mother.

Kitten licked one shoulder. She heard a voice call faintly, "Marigold!" A wisp of a cat streaked from the hall toward the hearth, saw Kitten and paused, fluffing up what must once have been a magnificent calico coat.

Kitten yawned and licked the other shoulder. She didn't think this wisp could or would harm her. "Marigold!" came the faraway cry again. The calico sneered at Kitten and jumped over her, leaving a trail of cold air. She too floated out of view up the aperture.

Kitten thought for a moment, then walked into the fireplace. Cool ashes felt silky on the pads of her feet but she was careful to avoid the still warm heart of yesterday's fire.

She looked up the chimney.

1

"April Fools," Gerry groaned, feeling daunted by the pile of bills on her desk. She'd paid some, laid others aside. The oil bill, for example. Almost $1,000 every time the tank was filled, and, over the long, hard Quebec winter, the first of which she'd just survived, several tanks had been delivered.

She remembered the jolt with which she'd woken last fall, when the first delivery had been made: the clunk as the hose pipe nozzle was dropped into the metal receptacle at the side of the house where her bedroom was; then the eerie shriek of the oil being forced in. Then more clunking as the delivery man removed the nozzle.

She'd been drifting off to sleep when the sound of the front screen door slapping shut woke her again.

She'd gone down to investigate, opened the inside front door and retrieved a folded green bill. "Eight-hundred and seventy-four dollars!" she'd said and been unable to return to sleep from the shock of the amount.

Now, three such bills had been paid and she was glumly looking at the fourth, along with those for her phone, electricity and credit cards.

"If only they *were* jokes. Bob, help!"

The sleek black tuxedo cat sitting on her desk opened his eyes, then blinked slowly. "Not in my job description," his lazy purr seemed to say.

She pushed the bills away. "Not in your job description, accounting, eh?" She chucked him under the chin.

Bob looked surprised, whether from the chucking or the fact that she was finally starting to connect with his thoughts the way even the six-month-old kitten could.

Gerry did it again. "Where is Jay, anyway? I don't want to shut her in here again."

Bob sat up and groomed. He didn't care what happened to that little pipsqueak; trying to play with his white whiskers or the white tip of his black tail whenever he dozed off. Then he relented, allowed his gaze to flick to a corner of the cramped little office.

Gerry got up and peered behind the tall, old-fashioned wooden filing cabinet. The kitten, crouched before a crack in the wainscotting, looked up. Gerry edged around the cabinet and picked it up by its shoulders. Its body stretched long and lean. "My, you're growing," Gerry said, and laughed at the cobwebs that festooned the little black head. "It looks like you're wearing a veil, Jay. Are you going out?" She removed the webs and dust and cuddled the kitten.

It set up an immediate loud purring, casting a satisfied glance at Bob. He nonchalantly took in the scene, fully aware that nothing and no one could dislodge him from top place in Gerry's affections. "I'm hungry," his mistress announced. She picked up her empty coffee cup and they trooped downstairs, adding the odd cat to their procession as they moved toward the kitchen.

The cats had been fed their suppers hours ago, when Gerry had arrived home from work around four, but they were still interested in what she might be having. "I'm so tired," she moaned, standing in front of the open fridge. "Suppose I just—" She'd been going to say "order a pizza" when the phone rang. "If it's a telemarketer, I'll ask them what's for supper."

She put on a silly voice. "Well, hello there," she chirped.

"Well, hello there back," Doug Shapland chirped in response. "How did it go?"

She sighed with relief. "It went. My last class. Done. Did you eat?"

"No. That's why I'm calling."

"I was just going to order a pizza."

"I'll pick it up," he offered.

"Okay. See you."

"See you soon," he said warmly.

Gerry rushed upstairs, washed and changed. She took a deep breath and looked in the mirror. She saw a little person in her twenties wearing comfy grey sweats, with freshly brushed long red hair and a face shining with anticipation. Doug was coming! They'd only been together for — what? — less than two months. She remembered their first "date," going to the Lovering theatre to see a play with songs from the Second World War. Surprising herself, she'd enjoyed it. She ran downstairs and was laying out plates and glasses when he arrived.

She met him at the door with a hug, which he was unable to reciprocate with the pizza box balanced on one hand and a plastic bag in the other. Gerry took the bag and looked in. "Brownies! And chips!"

He grinned, his thin face animated. "I like your enthusiasm. Makes me feel young. Anyway, we're celebrating the end of you having to drive to work twice a week in all kinds of weather, as well as the end of winter."

She looked out the kitchen window at the snowy driveway and bare trees. "End of winter, huh? Are you sure?"

He frowned. "Well, we could get more snow. I remember once we had a two-day blizzard at the end of April and — " He was stopped by the look of horror on Gerry's face. "I sound like an old codger, don't I?" He put on a mock quavery voice. "That was the year of the Great Easter Snow." He switched back to being Doug. "Don't worry. That year, two weeks later, we were in shorts planting peas. Hungry?"

"Famished." They carried the feast into the living room and sat at the big table. For a while there was nothing but the sounds of eating. The cats came to see Doug and receive his greetings and pats. As handyman to their previous owner, Gerry's Aunt Maggie, who'd left them and the house, The Maples, to Gerry almost a year ago, Doug was well known to most of the felines. And since he and Gerry had been seeing each other, he'd been a more frequent visitor. Of medium height and build, and an artist, he'd had a hard life. Married Gerry's cousin Margaret when they were both too young, had three children too quickly, one after the other, been given a job he didn't like by his wife's father, and drowned his frustrations in alcohol abuse, from which he was recovered — or so he, his family and friends hoped.

"So tell me about your last day," he urged.

Gerry, who'd just taken a massive bite of a brownie, chewed and swallowed quickly. "Oh, it was nice. The kids were nice. They felt sorry for Luc — he hobbled in using a cane — and glad term is almost ended. I taught the first half of the class, so he could see where we'd got up to, then he taught the second. He's much more experienced than I am. He hardly looked at his notes."

"He had two months to study them," Doug commented. Luc Sauze had been meant to teach art history at the local college for the full term, but had had a serious car crash before term began. Gerry, hoping for occasional substitute work to supplement her earnings from commercial art, had turned up at the right time to replace him.

She sighed.

"Sad?" Doug queried.

She shook her head. "Not *sad* sad, but, you know, sad I won't see the kids anymore. I'll miss the money, that's for sure. You won't believe how much my latest oil bill is."

Doug, who heated with wood and electricity, nodded sympathetically. "I hear you." He brightened. "Since I'm cutting down on the cigarettes, I'm saving money."

"Good for you," Gerry said encouragingly. "I know it's difficult." She continued, "I'll even miss the drive. The river road is so interesting."

"You can still drive on it."

"But I won't. Not so much. I'll stay at home and work. It's different."

"You don't have to tell me," Doug replied cheerfully. An artist himself, but responsible for his three almost adult sons — James, Geoff Jr., and David — he rarely had time for random drives or his art, working any odd jobs that presented. Since Gerry had met him a year ago, he'd been a bartender, boat-restorer, gardener and handyman.

Gerry felt contrite. Unlike him, she had domestic help and she employed a part-time gardener-handyman — Doug. And she was working in her chosen field. "Oh, Doug, I didn't mean — I mean — how is the piece?"

"The piece" was a large neon sculpture Doug had been working on in secret all winter. Gerry had only found out about it by accident when Doug's youngest son David had casually made reference to it when Gerry had been at their house. She hadn't seen it and Doug said, at the slow rate he was going, it might be no one ever would.

"The trouble is," he began, "I keep changing it. It won't stay still." He closed the pizza box. The cats, who knew this signalled the end of the feast, collectively relaxed. Nothing for them. Fine. Most of them drifted away.

Gerry moved to the sofa and gently displaced a few cats. She tried a weak joke. "Well, that's neon for you. Always in flux. Har."

Doug still seemed dejected. He followed her and flopped down. "Plus, James will be finished classes next week and Geoff and David next month, and then it'll be back to driving them around or worrying what they're up to all summer." They cuddled for a moment.

"I'm really glad you got this sofa," he murmured. "I wouldn't like to try this if we were sitting in the rocking chairs."

"Do you, um, have to rush off tonight?"

He smiled at her hopeful face. "No, actually. I have nowhere I have to be, except here. What do you suggest?"

Much, much later, as he quietly came downstairs and prepared to leave, putting on his jacket by the living room hearth, he noticed the kitten, standing in cold ash, looking up the chimney.

2

Gerry rolled over, feeling deliciously warm. "Doug?" she murmured and reached out. Her fingers encountered cat fur and then four paws closed on her hand.

She stifled a shriek. She lifted the covers and peered at the cat. "Jay! No! No claws!" She pulled the protesting kitten out from its warm nest and into daylight.

It turned its attention to Bob, sprawled on Gerry's second pillow. Bob's ears flattened. Before the situation could escalate, Gerry sat up and swung her legs onto the floor. Jay, distracted, leapt on her slippers. Gerry slipped them on, then indulged the kitten in a mock battle with her feet.

"Hey, Jay, aren't you hungry for breakfast? I am." She picked up the little cat, which switched on its noisiest purr. Accompanied by Bob and Lightning (a shy tortoiseshell who'd been scared out of the room as soon as Jay's nonsense had begun, but who usually slept at the foot of Gerry's bed), she made her way downstairs.

Cats fed and their litter boxes emptied, she sat at the living room table, sipping her coffee, looking out at the lake.

Free! She was free! Well, comparatively. She still had her once-a-week drawing class to give but that was here at the house and, unlike most of the art history students at the college, these students *wanted* to attend.

No more preparing lectures, marking essays and presentations. She made a second coffee and thought carefully. What did she *really* want to do?

Obviously, she had to continue maintaining the house and the cats. So that meant she couldn't give up creating her daily comic strip *Mug the Bug* or the greeting cards that had spun off from the strip's main character.

She'd finished her children's book *The Cake-Jumping Cats of Dibble* and, on being informed how saturated the market for children's books was, had resolved on self-publishing. As long as she made *some* money it would be worthwhile. Right?

She'd decided to donate half of the profits to a local cat rescue agency. They set themselves up in malls and community centres with cages of cats up for adoption and had suggested Gerry join them to promote the book. That should be fun. She hoped.

So what else? She thought of the one painting she'd done in March. *Night Crossing*, she called it, and it was a departure from her other usually humorous work.

She went into the dining room and greeted some of the cats sitting there. Blackie and Whitey, a fluffy sister-brother pair, one black, one pale beige, were snuggled on the chair nearest the door to the room where Gerry hung her art. "Aw, aren't you guys cute?" She caressed them, then went into the gallery.

Night Crossing hung alone on one wall of the small room. Two wolves paused, eyes on the onlooker, as they traversed the frozen river. Behind them, on the far shore, the distant spire of a church rose above the lights of a village. Ahead of them and up a rise was a snowy road. The whole scene, she hoped, was slightly ominous as well as beautiful.

Jay entered the room and gazed at a portrait of a young girl that hung on another wall. She sat and licked a shoulder, then looked at the drawing again.

Gerry picked her up and let her sniff the frame. "We think that's my Great-Great Aunt Margie, Jay. She was born in this house and lived here for a long time."

Jay put out a paw to the portrait. Gerry stepped back. "I don't trust your claws, you little monkey." She kissed the kitten's velvety black head.

The kitten struggled and Gerry released it. It scampered from the room. Gerry looked again at the wolves framed by majestic old trees and shrubs near the shore. What if she painted a spring scene of the lake with some other wild animal in it?

She thought of last fall, of the masses of wild geese on the lake. Last summer she'd been enchanted by the great blue herons that slowly walked in the shallows. But spring? What would she see in spring? As if on cue a blue jay called and landed on the window sill. Nice, but —

She would ask Doug. Or Prudence. Or Cathy or Blaise or Andrew — any of her neighbours and friends would know. Or just wait and see. Rabbits?

When the phone rang, she answered it eagerly. But it wasn't any of her friends. It was the veterinary hospital, reminding her that Jay, who'd already had her first vaccinations, was due to be spayed.

Gerry took a deep breath. "And when I bring her in, could I also bring one or two of the other cats for their shots?" They fixed a time on Saturday. After she hung up, she stared idly out the kitchen window towards the empty house next door.

Recently, there'd been some activity over there. Tradesmen's vans had been coming and going and the contractors Gerry used for her snow removal and the big maintenance jobs Doug couldn't do — the Hudsons — had been on the property cutting and trimming trees. She wondered who the new owners could be. "Must have money," she murmured and thought about how she was going to pay for nineteen cats to have their annual checkups.

She reached for the phone again and called the auction house that was handling the sale of her painting by Paul-Émile Borduas. Yes, all was in preparedness for the auction. It would be the following Tuesday. Would she be attending? They would expect her.

Okay, she thought. Money out. Money in. A lot of money in, hopefully, if someone loved the Borduas her Aunt Maggie had casually left her to discover hanging in the house. "Then I'll insulate the roof and walls and get a wood stove and go on vacation," she announced breathlessly to the assembled half-dozen cats in the living room. She added, "Now, who wants to go to the vet first?" No one volunteered.

She went upstairs and checked the voluminous files her aunt had kept containing the cats' information. She sorted through by date and compiled a list, then groaned. "Lightning. Lightning would be first." She went back downstairs.

The cat in question, a tortoiseshell with a stub of a tail and big scars down her back legs, was lurking in a corner of the living room while a group of cats relaxed by the fireplace. Bob adorned Gerry's work table. "Only two cat carriers and I'm assuming no one wants to share with Lightning?" Lightning's stumpy tail twitched angrily as she skittered sideways out of the room. "Sorry," Gerry called after her, "but you know it's true." She turned to address Mother. "Mother, would you like to come with Jay to the vet?" Mother blinked her acquiescence.

Gerry rummaged on the table. She decided she would ignore the various work piles there. "Ah! Here it is." She pulled a rocker over to the sunlight by the window and flipped through the exercise book that contained Aunt Maggie's childhood efforts at writing. "Stories of Lovering: True and Imagined" had been compiled when Maggie had been about ten. She wrote about local characters with the breathtaking honesty of a child.

Gerry looked for a story she hadn't yet read and settled on "The Singing Milkman." At the back of her mind, the tiny seed of an idea for another children's book, or maybe books, was germinating.

Every morning (except Sunday) the milkman would get up before anybody else. He'd harness his horse to his wagon and drive to the dairy. When he got to the dairy, he'd sing "Milkman here. Where's my milk?" just loud enough that the dairy workers would hear and bring him the milk for delivery. He'd sing "Thank you," before heading out to work.

He had a very deep, very rich voice. "Like the cream at the top of the bottle of milk," people would say.

He was a very tall man with a very long face and long skinny fingers.

His horse was a bay mare named Lady B. She had a little white star on her forehead between her eyes, and a sour expression. Perhaps she didn't enjoy the milkman's singing.

Gerry smiled as she envisioned the peevish bay mare. What would be the angle for such a book of stories? What would make people like it? The stories were all set in the first half of the twentieth century. Was local history the answer? The people of Lovering were very proud of and interested in who and what had gone before in their little town. They would buy such a book for their children and grandchildren but the adults would read it too.

For hours every morning Lady B and the milkman delivered milk to the people of Lovering; Lady B clip-clopping along, her ears twitching backwards, and the milkman singing.

He sang every type of song: hymns, folk tunes, songs from the radio. And when he stopped at people's homes and placed their orders on their porches or inside cunning little cupboards cut into a wall that could be opened from the inside, he'd sing, for example: "Two quarts of milk, one pound of butter. Two quarts of milk. One pound of butter," if that was their order.

And the people still abed heard the singing of the milkman outside their homes and knew their milk had arrived and they really should get up and bring it inside. And most of them liked the singing. But some of them did not.

Gerry stopped reading and jotted down a list of the scenes she could draw so far. If history was to be the key, she'd need photos of Lovering. Would the local newspaper have a file?

She ate something, then decided, as she'd be at the vets the next day, to do some grocery shopping.

The snow really was melting. Or was it just packing down? Both, she observed, looking at the dirty layers revealed in the piles either side of her parking pad.

She patted the Mini's hood affectionately. She'd had her fears when daunting amounts of snow had fallen, but the diminutive car had proved indomitable, surviving being crushed under a tree and sliding into a ditch.

She drove past the little church and churchyard where her parents and other relatives were buried, past the church hall, over the tracks and down the hill into Lovering.

She decided to walk around before shopping and parked near the little shop where she often found gifts. It had been closed for most of the winter. She wondered if they had new stock on display. She opened the door and looked around eagerly — and ran right into her Aunt Mary.

Both women took a step back. To Gerry, the background noise in the shop — the murmur of customers, the friendly bickering between the couple who owned the store, the classical music that sweetened the atmosphere — faded. She became aware of her own breathing, felt her heart pound. She looked into her aunt's eyes, expecting to see hostility or misery or loneliness.

She was surprised instead to see triumph and her aunt's lips curving. Mary almost looked *glad* to see her.

Gerry cleared her throat nervously. "Er, how are you, Aunt Mary?"

Mary said nothing but her eyes narrowed and Gerry was reminded of cats' eyes before the pounce. Her aunt jerked her head toward the back of the store where a large room smelling of potpourri and full of lamps, pillows, and pretty dishes and ornaments opened out. In a daze, Gerry followed. Last time she'd met her aunt in public, the woman had cut her dead. Whatever she wanted, it couldn't be good.

They paused by a display of dishes and tea towels with a seashell motif. Aunt Mary casually picked up a decorative plate.

Gerry tried again. "Are you well, Aunt?" She wished she could like this relative. After all, she was her father's and Aunt Maggie's sister, the middle child, the last one surviving. And a recent widow.

Her aunt put down the plate and unfolded a tea towel. "Whoever would want this?" she asked, her voice dripping with scorn.

Gerry didn't know why, but she had an urge to defend the tea towel and shell-lovers in general. "What did you want to discuss, Aunt Mary?"

Her aunt strolled over to a floral display. "These are rather nice." She flicked a well-lacquered index finger against a mug covered with pink roses.

The cup gave out a tiny ping and Gerry felt sorry for it. "Yes," she agreed doubtfully. "Only a few months before we see the real—"

"Margaret's getting out," Mary said with a smile and moved to the next display, objects with childlike themes of teddy bears, bunnies and balloons.

Gerry stayed where she was. She couldn't believe she'd heard correctly. Margaret was getting *out*? Last she'd heard, her cousin — Mary's daughter — was in a secure facility, ostensibly for her own protection.

"I've been visiting her all winter," Mary added. "Coaxing her to talk, to get well." She picked up a tiny mug with baby rabbits skipping around its girth and smiled at it. "I've convinced the doctors to release her into my care."

Gerry's mouth dropped open. Margaret's doctors must be blind! Releasing a mentally unstable person into Mary's custody made as much sense as releasing a...a...a kitten to a wolf! "But I thought — "

Her aunt stepped close to Gerry, her fingers gripping the bunny mug. Her voice hissed. "You thought you could influence first my husband and then my son to incarcerate" — her voice shook — "to incarcerate my daughter in a mental home and leave her to rot. And you thought I'd just accept this?" She took another step closer to Gerry, who was now only inches away. Her eyes glittered. "And you thought you'd take her ex-husband and her sons while you were at it. Was that why you did it? Eh? Eh?"

Gerry looked around nervously. Aunt Mary's voice had been rising in intensity and people were beginning to look, even edge away from where they stood. She wondered what exactly her aunt was accusing her of. She inhaled deeply and breathed out. "Uncle Geoff — " she began.

Aunt Mary bared her teeth and made an exasperated noise. "Him? Worthless! Chose to believe you, your insinuations, over his own daughter!"

Gerry realized she couldn't tell her aunt about Geoff Petherbridge's letter, residing in her safety deposit box, in which he recounted the sad unravelling of his daughter's mind when she confessed to the murder of Aunt Maggie. Couldn't tell her in this public space, anyway. She fought for calmness. What would this mean for Doug? For his sons? For Margaret?

"So she'll be staying with you?"

Mary seemed disappointed by this practical question. She took a step back and put down the bunny cup. "Yes. The doctors think if she's at home with me, without the burden of looking after the boys, it will be — " She seemed at a loss for words. "Better," she concluded.

"Better for who?" Gerry said softly, picking up a pretty white mug with matching lid, decorated with scarlet poppies, and moving swiftly to the cash.

She sat in her car, trembling. This can't be happening, this can't be happening, was all she could think. Eventually, she was reminded of the groceries she needed, reversed the car and drove to the store.

As she walked up and down the aisles, trying to concentrate on her list, on prices, a worried voice inside her head kept asking, "How is this going to affect Doug? And me?"

When she got home, she couldn't settle. She wanted to talk about Margaret. But with whom? Andrew, Margaret's brother? Presumably, he was fine with the idea of releasing her. But how could he be? Uncle Geoff had written his son a letter before his suicide. Gerry, who hadn't read that letter, wondered, could Uncle Geoff have been too vague? Had he not spelled out the seriousness of Margaret's obsession? Her need to please her mother? Who alternately praised and undermined her.

Gerry phoned the one person who had exactly the same information as she: her housekeeper, Prudence.

"Thank you for giving me last Thursday off," Prudence said.

"Oh, you're welcome, Prudence. I know you have other clients and a personal life as well." Silence at the other end. Gerry continued. "Anyway, the cats aren't going outside yet so the floors don't get as dirty. Though there are a lot of fur balls rolling around."

"Wait until May and June, when they all start shedding at once. What's up?"

Gerry related the painful conversation she'd just had with Mary, concluding with, "Are those doctors insane? Releasing Margaret to the very person who's the cause of her problem?"

Prudence sensibly replied, "We don't know. They may have diagnosed a mental illness and be treating it successfully."

"Oh. I hadn't thought of that." Gerry paused. "But still, you and I know there's a very good reason for not letting her be at large."

"Yes. But nobody else does. What if Andrew thinks Margaret's only a danger to herself? And Mary's so self-centred, it would never occur to her that her supervision could be anything but beneficial."

"Do you think I should talk to Andrew?"

"Definitely. Feel him out, how much he knows. And we should wait and see what Margaret's like now before we judge her."

"But she — " Gerry hesitated, not wanting to say the words over the phone. "She — you know…"

"Do you think I can ever forget?" Prudence sounded exasperated. Then she continued in a calmer voice, "I'll see you on Monday and we'll talk it through then."

Gerry didn't sleep well that night. How should she approach Andrew about his sister's mental instability? Did Doug know his ex-wife, the mother of his three sons, was about to re-enter their lives? How would Margaret's return affect his relationship with Gerry?

To make matters worse, Jay was also restless, or maybe just reacting to Gerry's emotions. The kitten flitted about the bedroom, jumping on and off the furniture, knocking a few items off the mantelpiece then pouncing on them.

She jumped onto Gerry's pillow several times, tickling her nose with her whiskers, trying to get under the covers, wiggling once she did, then resurfacing, irritating Gerry's eyes with her twitching tail.

It was after midnight when Gerry gave up on sleep. She would snack or make tea or work. Yes. Work. That always made her feel better.

She carried Jay downstairs and put on the kettle. She would try out her new cup. The lid ensured her tea wouldn't cool when she worked. Bob and Lightning had remained deeply asleep on her bed. While she waited for the kettle to boil, she ate a cookie and followed Jay around the downstairs of the house.

The kitten paused by the hearth, standing in the ashes; seemed to be curious about the dark vertical hole up which she peered.

Gerry picked her up, dusting off her little feet. "That's a chimney, Jay. Where the smoke goes."

The kitten jumped down and trotted into the dining room where many cats slept on chairs around the massive wooden table. Jay sat between two chairs looking up. Harley slept on one chair, Kitty-Cat on the other. Jay mewed.

From the hall came a crash. "That sounded like a picture!" Gerry exclaimed. When she got to the large foyer, she saw that the portrait of her ancestor John Coneybear had slipped from its place hanging over a small table. Fortunately the table had broken its fall and both were undamaged. "It can't have been a cat," Gerry informed Jay, "unless it was leaping through the air." The nail that held the painting up was bent down. The portrait must have just slipped off.

Gerry leaned the painting against the wall. Had he been a bad man? She knew a few things and suspected a few more that led her to think that had been the case.

Jay was cowering at Gerry's feet. Gerry turned her back on the portrait and addressed the kitten. "Jay. How about I warm up some milk for you? Would you like that? Would it help you to sleep?"

Behind her came a sharp crack. She turned to see the portrait face down on the table. I must have positioned it on a bad angle, she thought. The kitten gave a cry and ran from the room.

Gerry followed her. Jay now stood, meowing, in the living room in front of the cupboard door behind which lived the vacuum cleaner. "All right, all right, no one's going to threaten you with the vacuum at this time of night." Gerry remembered that that was where she'd found Marigold, her beloved calico cat, the morning she died, and felt a pang of sorrow.

Bob stalked into the room, fur bristling, while Lightning slunk in behind him. Jay and Gerry's restlessness must have transmitted itself to them. The two cats joined Jay in staring at the cupboard door. Gerry could hear the kettle was almost boiling. "Well, now that you're all here, I'll just open the cupboard and show you nothing's — "

A cold breeze blew from the fireplace to the cupboard door. The door opened with such force it banged against the wall. Bob, standing on the hearth rug, his eyes huge and his fur puffed, leapt to one side, growling. Lightning, crouched in a corner, closed her eyes and hunkered down. The kettle screamed. Gerry scooped up the quailing kitten and slammed the door shut. "Enough!" she shouted.

Bob's fur settled back down. He groomed on the rug. Lightning trotted out of the room. And, in Gerry's arms, the kitten began to purr.

3

"I don't know what happened to my cats last night," Gerry remarked to the elderly woman whose tired old dog sat on the floor panting. "It was like they'd all decided to go crazy at the same time."

An excited border collie entered the veterinary hospital, yanking its owner from side to side.

The woman replied, "I had a friend who used to breed dogs and she said 'One dog is a pet. Two dogs are on the way to becoming a pack.' With a pack mentality, I guess she meant. How many cats do you have, anyway?" She leaned over and looked in the carrying cases. "One, two, three. Yes, that's quite a few. I've only ever had one dog at a time but this is my seventh. In a row. So I guess you could say I've owned a lot of dogs. The one before this one, no, I lie, it was the one before that…"

Gerry let her mind go blank. She smiled and nodded. She didn't usually tell strangers that she had nineteen cats. Let the nice woman think she had only these three. And she was glad the woman hadn't said something like, "Perhaps they're sensitive. Perhaps they're seeing ghosts." Because that's what it had felt like to her. The cats seemed to be seeing things that weren't there.

"Funny creatures, cats and dogs," the woman was saying. "If they know you're upset they react in two ways. I had a dog who would run away and hide whenever I got emotional — you know, cried. And another dog, a smaller one, who would creep close to me in sympathy, it felt like."

Gerry turned her full attention to the woman. "I was upset. I'd just received some bad news and couldn't sleep."

"Well," the woman said triumphantly. "There you are. They were just reacting."

"Rocco Storey?" an attendant called.

"That's us," the woman said. "Good luck with your cats. Come on, Rocco." Rocco got to his feet and padded slowly away.

Gerry picked up the carrier containing Lightning and put it on her lap. She felt the cat's weight shift. "It's okay, Lightning. It'll be okay."

The last time Gerry had sat in this waiting area, she'd been covered in the blood of her neighbour's cat and wondering how the poor thing could possibly survive its injuries. It had, but with a heck of a scar.

A different attendant appeared with a sheaf of papers. "Coneybear? Three cats?"

"That's us," Gerry called. The girl made as if to take the carrier off Gerry's lap. "I'll keep this one, I think," Gerry said. The girl picked up the box containing Mother and Jay. As they passed the collie, it lunged. Lightning hissed. Then they all filed into a tiny room.

"Dr. Perry will be with you shortly." Gerry was alone with her pets. Jay first, then Mother, then Lightning, she thought. I hope the vet has experience with savage cats. She opened the door on Mother and Jay's box. First, curious Jay, then stately Mother stepped out onto the examining table. The vet entered.

A portly man with a calm demeanour, he took in the two cats and Gerry's worried face. "Who do we have here?"

"This one is to be spayed. This one is for shots. And this one — " She lifted Lightning's box onto the table and Lightning hissed. "This one needs an attitude adjustment."

The vet peered at Lightning. "Oh, I remember you," he said, adding, "Where's Miss Coneybear?"

"Well, I suppose I'm Miss Coneybear but perhaps you are referring to my Aunt Maggie Coneybear. She died last year. And left me the cats. I was here a little while ago but saw Dr. Morin."

"Oh. I'm sorry. I didn't know. So you're the lucky new lion tamer. How many is it? Twenty?"

"Nineteen." She indicated Jay. "And this is the newest."

The vet stuck his head out the door of the room. "I'm going to need help," he called. When the vet tech came, he handed her Jay. "I'll spay this one at the end of the day. Come right back," he said as the girl took Jay away. Gerry felt her throat tighten as Jay's little face looked at her over the technician's shoulder.

The vet stroked Mother and referred to the file. "Let's see. Not yet ten." He looked at her teeth, felt her throat and took her temperature. "The usual shots. She looks fine." He was quickly finished with Mother and she was easily returned to the box that Gerry put on the floor.

She placed Lightning's cage on the table and opened the door. A low growling issued from inside. The vet waited. The technician reappeared wearing long leather gauntlets. The vet suddenly seized the box and tipped it on its end, the open door swinging.

They all bent over to peer inside. Lightning was clinging to the grill work on the sides of the box with her claws. "Go ahead, Belle," sighed the vet. The technician inserted first one then another protected hand into the cage. The growling intensified, now going up the scale, now down.

Half of Lightning — the rear half — appeared in Belle's hands. "Can you?" she asked the vet. He sighed again and grasped Lightning's rear legs in one large hand.

"I've got the box," Gerry offered and the vet added a second hand to controlling half a cat. The technician pushed her whole arm in the cage, finally dislodging the cat's claws from the grill. Lightning appeared on the table, her jaws clamped around one of the girl's protected fingers. Gerry removed the cage and Belle applied pressure to the struggling beast.

The vet unfolded a towel slowly. "I always liked your aunt. She was a brave woman." He slipped the towel around Lightning, compressing her limbs, leaving only her head exposed. "Of course," he joked, "if you were a real tiger, we'd anaesthetize you before any treatment."

Lightning growled deep in her throat, the pitch varying from ultrahigh to extra low.

Between them, the vet and technician managed some kind of examination. The vet tsk-tsked when he saw the hindquarters. "Probably burned," he suggested. "We don't know. She was healed when your aunt adopted her. She may have been tortured and that would account for the PTSD."

Gerry was aghast. "I just thought she was difficult. Do you often see cases where animals have been tortured?"

"Not often." He poked a thermometer into Lightning and they all held their breath. But the cat seemed stunned and was still. "About once a month, maybe, not including puppy mill dogs."

"Are there kitten mills, too?" Gerry asked.

"Oh yes," he replied. "Are you interested in cat rescue?" First one and then the other of the cat's shoulders was exposed and her shots given.

"I'm supposed to volunteer at cat adoption events. As a local artist and soon-to-be author of—uh—a cat-related children's book. I'm giving them half the profits."

"That's good of you. One, two, three." With Gerry holding the box steady, Belle pushing and Dr. Perry whipping the towel off Lightning at the last minute, they reinserted her into her cage.

"Yay!" Gerry said. "Do you get many like her?"

Belle smiled. "About one a day. How did you get her into the cage at home?"

"Wrapped in a tea towel." They giggled. "And I put the cage up high on a shelf so she had to get in or fall."

Dr. Perry washed his hands. "I'll check with my partner, but I think it will be okay with her if you want to display copies of your book here."

"Oh, how kind. Thank you very much." So focused on Lightning was she that Gerry forgot Mother quietly sitting in the second cat carrier and had to go back to the examining room when Belle called her.

She paid and made appointments for a few more cats the following week. She was to pick up Jay the next day. "We're open till two on Sunday," the receptionist said.

The house was quiet when she got home. She opened the doors of the two cat carriers and watched. Mother came out sedately enough, sniffing around the corners of the living room before settling on the hearth rug, as if she'd decided to wait for Jay there. Gerry kneeled on the rug and petted the big marmalade cat. "Good girl, Mother. You know I'll bring Jay back tomorrow. Well, you don't know, but you trust me." She bent over to look at Lightning, still in her box. "Which is more than this one does." Gerry sucked her lips coaxingly. Nothing. Lightning looked balefully out at her. "Well, I'm hungry. Time for lunch."

She made a sandwich — tuna for a change from her usual ham and cheese — and heated up some chicken noodle soup. She ate in the living room at the table facing the lake.

It was a dull day but light reflecting off snow and ice made it seem bright. She watched as bits of ice broke off and floated down river and remembered one of her father's favourite stories. How he and neighbour kids would put on their rubber boots in the spring, go down to the shore and out onto the remaining attached ice. They'd jump up and down so smaller bits would break off, then try to ride the bits. Icebergs, they'd called them.

Inevitably someone would fall in or lose a boot, or both, and the game would be called off. Kids aren't allowed to play such dangerous games anymore, Gerry mused. I should call Doug. She spoke to his answering machine. "Hey, it's me. I wondered what you're doing tonight. Bye."

Her eye was drawn to the orchid her friend Bea had given her for her birthday. Safely ensconced on the mantelpiece where only Bob ventured, some of its purple-splotched white petals were starting to brown and curve inwards. She phoned Bea. No reply. She left her message. "So, Bea, the orchid is looking a bit tired. Am I killing it? Help!"

She pulled out *Mug the Bug* and did a strip. Then another. Mug, almost invisible on the page, had somehow joined a choir. Possibilities for nonsense ensued. Mug tickling other choristers' noses; being inhaled and almost swallowed; singing loudly and out of tune but never getting caught. It was foolish fun.

She drank coffee and fed the cats. She got hungry and phoned Doug again. "Hello. Hope everything is okay. Call me." She chewed at a bit of loose skin on one finger. This was Doug's pattern: when things got complicated, he pulled away. Was that what was happening? He must know by now that Margaret was getting out. Mary had no self-editing mechanism; she might have babbled the news to any of her grandsons James, Geoff Jr. or David, and they would have told their father.

Maybe Margaret was already at Mary's house. Maybe they were all over there now. Maybe Doug would feel he had to support her in her recovery. Maybe —

"Ick," Gerry said aloud. "He's unselfish but he's not self-destructive. I'm getting carried away, cats. How about a cozy fire?"

Warmer days meant the furnace went on less frequently so, strangely, the house was cooler in spring and fall than in winter. And damp. A fire would be just the thing. Then she'd think about supper.

By the time the fire was crackling, she'd decided to order BBQ chicken. As she was reaching for the phone, the front doorbell rang. "Who would use the front door?" she muttered. She twitched aside the curtain of a window next to the door and saw her cousin Andrew, who lived across the road, holding a large box.

"Hi, Andrew. Whatever have you got there?"

A tall man with a homely but nice face, he smiled and bent to kiss her cheek. "I have no idea but it's heavy. It must have been delivered when you were out."

"Come in by the fire. What can it be?" She inspected the label. "Bartle Printing. Bartle Printing! It's *Dibble*! It's my book!" She ran to get scissors and slit the top of the box.

They each took a copy. Andrew admired the cover. A castle nestled in a small wood. A parade of jaunty cats marched along a winding road toward it. "Wow. You must be so pleased. Your first book. I'm sure you'll write more. May I be the first to purchase a copy?"

Gerry was so happy, she kissed him again and gave him a hug. "Of course not! Have one for nothing!" She unpacked all 100 books and laid them in stacks on the table. Bob jumped up and sniffed the piles before dropping into the empty box. Gerry gloated. "This is so great! Now I can do a cat adoption event! And Dr. Perry, the vet, said I could leave a few copies at his office. Where else should I try to sell them, do you think?"

"Animal shelters, pet food and equipment stores, though they may want a cut."

"I'm giving half the profits to the cat rescue and adoption society. It's completely volunteer run." Bob crouched low in the box, emitting weird noises. Ronald, a thin white cat with a black moustache, became aware of him and crept up on the box.

"Well, in that case, maybe the stores will give you shelf space. Bookstores?"

"I looked into them. They want a big percentage. It would mean the cat adoption agency and I would only get a dollar each from each copy sold." The white tip of Bob's tail could be seen waving from within the box. Ronald was nearly there.

"Better than nothing. And they might be able to move them fast. Worth a shot."

"Thanks, Andrew. I forgot you must know a lot about marketing after running a store for most of your life."

Bob retracted his tail, there was a pause and Ronald leapt into the box as Gerry reached for it. She stared down at the two cats. They looked up at her rather foolishly. "You guys! Get out of there. I'm going to need this box to ferry books around in, not cats!" She tipped the box and first Ronald then Bob stepped out onto the floor with great dignity. "What? Us mess around in your precious box?" they seemed to be saying.

"Nothing about marketing books," Andrew replied cheerfully. "But the basics are the same." He was in the process of moving from owning the family's furniture store he'd managed with his late father, to design consulting.

Gerry blew cat hairs out of the box. "How's Markie?"

His face flushed happily. "She's great. Her turn to visit me next." Markie was the sister of their mutual friend and near neighbour Cathy Stribling, and lived in Arizona.

"Oh, I'd love to get together with you when she's here," Gerry said a trifle absently. She was fondling her books.

"I can see you want to be alone with them," Andrew joked. "I just figured you didn't know the package was there. Didn't want anyone to steal them overnight."

"Yes. Thanks, Andrew. Thanks so much." She'd closed the door on him and was adding wood to the fire when she remembered she should have spoken to him about his sister Margaret. "Rats!" Some of her pleasure in the shiny colourful books was diminished. Then she forgot everything else, including supper, as she spent the evening roughing out a marketing plan.

4

There were two important things Gerry knew she had to do that Sunday.

She reasoned that the longer Jay recuperated at the vets away from the temptation to play with her other cats, the better, so she made a few book-related phone calls before loading about fifty copies and an empty cat carrier into the car.

She drove first to the pet supplies store, took a deep breath and ten books, and marched toward the door. "They better display them; I must be close to their best customer," she muttered, thinking of all the treats, collars, nail clippers and other cat-related oddments she'd bought there over the last year.

She was enthusiastically welcomed. She bought a small bag of catnip and left ten books on the counter by the cash with a card that read: One half of the profits from the sale of this book go to benefit CRAS (Cat Rescue and Adoption Society). She also left an empty envelope for the money.

Outside in the car, she ticked off the store on a piece of paper and wrote "10 copies" and the date. "This is fun!" she told the Gerry in the rear-view mirror and drove to the next village where there was an animal shelter. They took ten copies as well, with the person on duty buying one right then and there for her granddaughter, she said, as she stuffed a twenty into the envelope and put the envelope in the till. She was kind enough to give Gerry a list of other shelters within an hour's drive. "I'm sure they'll all display them," she said helpfully. Gerry thanked her and left.

Back in the car, she added the list to the file, which said *Cats of Dibble* — Business on it. She drove a little ways to a bookstore and left one copy with the clerk for the absent manager to have a look at.

She scribbled "libraries" on a fresh sheet of paper. The time caught her eye. It was one already. She was hungry and the vet closed at two.

She drove to a drive-through and placed her order, then to the vets where she ate in the car — a hamburger, all dressed, and onion rings. Carefully wiping her fingers, she extracted ten copies of her book from the box and entered the vets. "I'm here to pick up Jay," she began, "and Dr. Perry said, if Dr. Morin agreed, I could display these here and you might sell them for me."

The receptionist disappeared for a few moments and Gerry sat down. She was the only client. She'd been so taken up with her book she'd forgotten Jay had just had a major operation.

The receptionist reappeared with Gerry's cat carrier. "Here she is," she said cheerily. "She'll be a bit sore for a while. Pick her up carefully and no vigorous play for a day or two."

Wondering who was going to communicate these instructions to the eighteen cats at home, Gerry peeked in at Jay who was curled up, blinking sleepily and, Gerry imagined, reproachfully at her. "Hello, little girl. I'm so sorry but it's for the best." She turned to the receptionist. "What do I owe you?" She paid the bill. "Uh, I have appointments for next Saturday, which I have to change. Can I move them to Friday? And did Dr. Morin say I could leave the books?"

"Yes and yes," the woman smiled. "I can't wait to read it."

In the first flush of gratified authorship, Gerry took her cat to the car and checked the vet hospital off her list. "Other vets" she scribbled on another piece of paper. She wedged Jay's box on the floor. "You're one of the very important things I have to do today," she cooed to the kitten. "Now for the other." And she drove to Doug's.

Bumping down his long narrow driveway, Gerry wondered what she'd do if she met his or another car. One of them would have to back up a long, long way. She guessed he had to pay someone to clear it of snow. It would take forever with a little handheld snow blower. But paying to clear a long driveway like this must be expensive — much more than the few hundred she handed over to the Hudsons to do hers.

She suddenly realized that she knew little really about Doug's day-to-day struggle to feed and clothe his sons, pay for their transportation and schooling and, in fact, maintain the small house where they lived. She knew Andrew helped out, paying for extras like sports, but that still left a lot of expenses for Doug to meet.

She parked. Doug's car wasn't there but that didn't mean he wasn't. With three sons in their late teens or early twenties, and only one car, it must be a case of tossing the keys from one driver to the other. She looked in at Jay. Asleep. She got out of her car with a copy of her book.

The house, originally a cottage, had been more than doubled in size by Doug when he'd been a young married man. He'd added a couple more bedrooms upstairs and extended the main floor into one big kitchen, dining and living room.

Gerry had been here infrequently. It only made sense that they'd have more privacy at her place, and anyway, she had a fairly bad memory of a hostile meeting with Margaret here. But she liked the house and its location in the woods, so far from the main road. She knocked on the door.

Someone pattered up the stairs behind her and rubbed her legs. "Hello, little Dee! Didi!" she cried. "Come to see your old mum?" She picked the kitten up. "You have a great playground here."

The door opened to reveal Doug's middle son, Geoff Jr. — tall, in his late teens, and with a look of his mother, Margaret.

"Hi, Geoff, I wonder — "

"Dad!" Geoff left her standing and went up the few stairs to the main floor. The kitten jumped out of Gerry's arms and followed him, mewing.

"Rude," muttered Gerry and shut the door. Doug, with a screwdriver in one hand and a wet rag in the other, came up from the basement. He looked surprised.

Gerry kissed him, leaning one hand on his chest. "You're soaked!"

Doug pulled at his wet shirt ruefully. "Sump pump woes. Don't ask. Coffee?"

They joined Geoff in the kitchen where he was scraping cat food out of a tin. The kitten purred loudly, moving back and forth near his feet.

Gerry sat at the kitchen table. "How are you, Geoff?"

"Fine," he mumbled, putting the cat's plate down on the floor.

"Imagine," she said brightly, "doing that nineteen times twice a day."

He grunted and put the tin in the fridge. Doug, making coffee, silently handed him a lid for the tin. Geoff jerked open the fridge door, laid the lid loosely over the open tin and slammed the fridge shut. "Hey!" Doug said sharply.

Gerry spoke. "I can't stay long. I've got Didi's sister in the car. Just picked her up from the vets after her operation. Has Didi been done yet?"

Doug nodded. "Coffee, Geoff?" His son grudgingly accepted a cup and turned to go upstairs. "Say goodbye to Gerry, Geoff," his father said gently.

"Bye, Gerry," the boy mumbled and left. They drank their coffee.

"Look. My book." He admired it for a moment but seemed preoccupied. Then she said, "I hadn't heard from you and the vet is close to your place so I thought — "

"Gerry." Doug covered her hand with his. "I know about Margaret. And I'm assuming you do too."

She nodded. "Doug, I'm worried. She's so hostile to me and, and —" She stopped. Doug didn't know his ex-wife was a murderer. Was this the moment when she'd have to tell him? It would probably mean going to the police with Uncle Geoff's letter. And what would Doug think of her for concealing this for the last few months? Sure, it was what Uncle Geoff had wanted, and Gerry had his letter to her in her safe deposit box to prove it. But there wasn't any evidence; the police wouldn't necessarily take the word of a dead man, or Gerry's recital of Margaret's angry confession to her just before her pathetic breakdown. Gerry quailed.

It was too much. She'd have to hope Aunt Mary could supervise her daughter.

Doug could see her obvious distress. "What? What?"

She gulped. "I'm just worried about you and the boys seeing Margaret. And…and…how it's going to make them hate me even more."

Doug said flatly, "*I'm* not going to see Margaret. I'm sure it wouldn't be good for her. Nor for me. The boys visit Mary occasionally. She still has her golf club and yacht club memberships and she likes to parade around with her grandsons there. So they'll see their mother with Mary present. And I'm divorced from Margaret. She divorced me. The boys are used to that. As for you and me —"

"If you say we should cool things down for a while, I'll divorce you! From being my boyfriend!" Gerry accompanied this threat by hitching her chair closer to his, putting her arm around him and snuggling. He smiled.

"No. I was going to say that I just won't stay the night anymore at your place. Until I see how Margaret is. If she drops in over here, I don't want the boys to have to deal with her on their own. Especially at night." He gave her a lingering kiss. "Mmm. Too bad Geoff's upstairs. We could —"

She opened her eyes and sighed. "Come over soon, okay?"

"Tomorrow?"

"Tomorrow Prudence will be cleaning."

"But she leaves at three or four, no?"

She kissed him again. "She leaves at three or four."

The woman in question arrived for work at 8:30 Monday morning, having cadged a ride from her neighbour. Of medium height and slight build, she was in her fifties. Her grey hair was pulled back in a little bun and her lips were thin. She was dressed in her usual attire: grey pants, a white shirt and a black sweater. Gerry, sipping her first coffee, noted the lack of a bag of baking ingredients with disappointment.

Since she'd met, or rather, re-met Prudence as an adult on an equal footing, Prudence had guided her through an informal course of baking. Beginning with the easy stuff like cookies, squares and cakes, they'd proceeded through pies to all the strange delicacies associated with Christmas: fruitcake, mince tarts; and Gerry had even made a trifle.

Then they'd moved on to scones and other tea party delights. Now when Gerry hosted her drawing class on a Wednesday afternoon, she selected and baked the refreshments herself. Nevertheless, she still felt disappointed and it must have shown on her face.

Prudence snapped open her ugly black purse and produced a little envelope that rattled when she shook it. "Seeds?" Gerry queried.

"In a way," her friend responded, "but not really." She handed Gerry the packet.

"Oh. Yeast." Gerry raised her eyes, now sparkling. "Are we going to make bread?"

Prudence shrugged, obviously pleased with Gerry's reaction but trying to make light of it. "If you want. We should start soon though. Bread takes at least half a day. I assume you have flour?"

Gerry produced it, along with the salt, sugar and oil Prudence demanded. "That's it?"

"That's it. Measuring cups and a big bowl. We're making two loaves — it's hardly worth bothering for just one — so three cups of warm water and one tablespoon of sugar, dissolved. Sprinkle the yeast and — no, don't stir it — walk away for a few minutes then come back."

Gerry washed the cat dishes from that morning's feed then returned to inspect her yeast. Prudence dried the dishes.

"Bubbles!"

"It's a living thing, now feeding on the sugar."

"Cool!"

"We can start adding the flour. The original recipe says six to eight cups but it can vary depending whether you use whole wheat or white or fifty-fifty. I usually just dump in three cups and a tablespoon of salt and then add flour by half cups until I've got a workable dough — one that won't stick too much to my fingers."

Gerry added and stirred and added and stirred until she had a stiff dough. "Now what?"

Prudence dipped her hand in the flour and threw a large quantity on the counter. "Now, we knead." She dumped the dough out onto the pile of flour, which puffed up. As she demonstrated the vigorous technique, more flour wafted around the area. "Now you. I've incorporated the remaining flour the recipe called for and the dough is workable. Now you want to knead for ten minutes while adding as little more flour as possible."

Gerry dived in. Looking at the clock, she was astonished to note, "That's only three minutes! I'm tired already."

"See how the dough is a nice smooth ball? Keep working it. It should be elastic by the time you're done."

Gerry carried on grimly. "Two more minutes." Then, "One minute." Then, "I'm done!"

Prudence meanwhile had washed the bowl. "Now I oil the bowl very lightly and put the dough back into it. Some people cover it with plastic wrap; I like to use a clean tea towel. Put it out of drafts — inside a cold oven is fine — and come back in one or two hours. I'm going to vacuum."

"Great! I'll clean up in here." When Gerry looked at the clock, she was surprised to see only a half an hour had passed. Huh. Another baking mystery simplified. She went away to work for a bit. Mug, of course. Had to do an episode a day to keep up. And she'd missed yesterday. She had one strip roughed out when the vacuum stopped and Prudence reappeared, beckoning.

When they opened the oven door, Gerry saw the bread had filled the bowl and pushed the cloth up. "Wow! Now what?"

"Now we punch it down, give it a light kneading on a floury surface and cut it in half. We could make buns with one lump if you like."

"No, let's just make two loaves: one for you and one for me."

"Okay. So now we're turning and folding under to make two neat balls. If you wanted round loaves you would put these on a greased baking sheet. But we'll use loaf pans this time.

"They look kind of small," Gerry noted doubtfully.

"Don't get ahead of yourself. Now, grease these pans and watch."

Gerry observed as Prudence shaped one ball into a loaf then knuckled it into the pan. She imitated her with the second ball.

Prudence re-covered the two loaf pans after they were put into the cold oven. "Now we wait again." Gerry went back to her cartoons while Prudence dragged the vacuum cleaner upstairs.

By the time Gerry was hungry for lunch, the dough had risen. "It looks like bread!" she remarked. They look the loaves out, heated the oven to 350 degrees and set the timer for twenty-five minutes. "I cannot believe how easy that was," Gerry said between bites of her grilled cheese sandwich and slurps of her split pea soup.

Prudence munched her peanut butter and pickle sandwich and offered Gerry her bag of potato chips. "To make a richer loaf, add an egg when the yeast has bubbled. Add grated cheese or raisins or other dried stuff when you're doing the first long kneading." An enticing baking bread smell permeated the area.

The oven timer pinged and they both got up. Gerry peered anxiously while Prudence tapped each loaf. "Does that feel and sound hollow to you?" she asked her pupil.

"Er, yes?" Gerry said doubtfully.

"I agree. Out they come. Right away out of the pans to cool on a rack. That's it. Bread."

They looked at their work proudly. "Coffee or tea?" Gerry asked.

"Just going to put the cat towels in the washer and lay down fresh ones. Tea, please."

Gerry made a pot and waited for Prudence. She poured them each a cup. "I don't have anything sweet," she apologized, "unless we eat the bread."

Prudence cautioned absently, "You'll get a sick stomach if you eat hot bread."

Gerry hesitantly asked, "Prudence, is this a good time to discuss Margaret?"

"Ah," her friend replied. "Actually, I have something more important to me to tell you about as well."

5

Gerry drove Prudence home. Well, Prudence drove, as she was studying for her driver's licence, but in Gerry's car. Then Gerry drove herself home.

Her friend Bea Muxworthy had returned her phone call that afternoon. "You're not killing it," Bea had answered her question about her tired-looking orchid. "It's just finishing its bloom period. It's been in bloom since your birthday. It's tired. Cut off the stem when the flowers are all done and give the plant some good light. If you're lucky it will re-bloom next year."

"Well, that's a relief," Gerry said. "What are you doing?"

"Going to a concert. A string quartet at the church. Want to come?"

"Er, no thanks. Classical music isn't my thing. And I'm expecting Doug later."

"Well, don't be a stranger," Bea had replied. "Since you've been seeing a certain handyman, we don't get together as much as we used to."

"I'm working like a madwoman, you know, besides seeing Doug. He's the one who's not often available. He has to work. I have to work." Gerry felt she was giving Bea a wrong impression, so added, "But it's going well.

"Good. Got to dash. Bye!" The idea of her friend, who suffered from multiple sclerosis, dashing, made Gerry smile, but if anyone with MS could dash, it would be Bea.

Doug also phoned that afternoon. He had a job to do, scraping a boat at the yacht club. He couldn't say no to the money and would be working into the evening. "I'm sorry, Gerry," he'd said.

She was disappointed. But it was just as well. What with the bread-making and talking with Prudence that afternoon, she hadn't gotten much drawing done. She would work that evening too.

When she got home she fed the cats. As the furry mass swirled around her ankles accessing their plates on the kitchen floor, Gerry made a coffee and stepped over and around them. She sat at the living room table, her hands under her jaw, and tried to make sense of what Prudence had told her.

Prudence had insisted they discuss Margaret first. She told Gerry that people had been talking about it in town already. "My friend Lucy phoned me yesterday to say it was being discussed after service at her church."

"But Prudence, what should we do?" Gerry had wailed. "We know she's dangerous. We just can't prove it."

"Keep well away," Prudence had advised bluntly. "Watch out and say nothing." She'd looked away and said, "Besides, I have other more pressing news, at least for me, personally."

Gerry sighed and leaned back, sipping her coffee. The cats, now mostly satisfied by their meat feed, were slowly entering the living room. The gluttons could be heard, still crunching kibble.

Bob jumped onto the table. Jay, who, after a sleepy day and night, had rebounded from surgery, followed suit. Min Min asked to be picked up. Mother purred by the hearth. Blackie and Whitey settled near her and dozed. Harley and Kitty-Cat emerged from the kitchen and paused to groom their enormous black and white bodies. The boys, three grey tiger-striped brothers, and their sidekick Ronald, ran out of the kitchen, stopped to take in the peaceful scene, then roared through into the next room. Other cats followed them at slower paces.

Prudence had told Gerry in a calm, unemotional voice that her ex-husband had contacted her, from prison, and wondered if he could see her. Gerry, not knowing anything about Prudence's marriage beyond her husband's name — Alexander Crick — had sat frozen, hoping her jaw wasn't gaping.

When Prudence had finished, Gerry had managed "Whatever you need: time off, for me to drive you somewhere, whatever."

Prudence had mused. "I just might take you up on the drive. I'll let you know. Right now, I need to dust this house."

Gerry looked down at a blank sheet of paper. She needed ideas for her comic strip. She needed funny ideas, yet she felt weighed down by the last few days' events.

She went into the kitchen and sliced the end off of her fresh loaf of bread. She slathered it with thin slices of cold butter and took a bite. Heaven! She knew what she was having for supper. She heated a can of comforting ravioli in tomato sauce. Double heaven!

As she ate, she wondered how Mug the Bug would manage in a bakery. Would he get rolled up in the dough and baked in the oven? Could she make it funny? She munched and scribbled, sketched and laughed, then decided the bread was so delicious to just have another slice of it for dessert. This time, as well as the butter, she added a large spoonful of Prudence's strawberry jam. Maybe she'd get Prudence to show her how to make jam this summer. Strawberry, raspberry, blueberry…Prudence. What would Prudence be doing by the summer? Would she be living with her husband? Would she still be Gerry's part-time housekeeper? What had he gone to prison for, anyway?

"Argh! Go back to work, woman," she urged herself. "All will be revealed. Eventually."

After working until late in the evening (and eating rather a lot of bread), then passing a restless night as the full moon traversed the night sky, alighting in first one window then another, Gerry got up early and drove to catch the train in Lovering.

The temperature was above zero, and an April shower made the snow-covered land steam. As she rode the train through agricultural, then suburban landscapes, the fog made shapes irregular and fuzzy.

In contrast, the interior of the train car and its occupants appeared sharp-edged, though muted. Funny how people on public transit seem paralyzed, she thought, and pulled out a small sketchpad from her knapsack and furtively captured a few faces. As they reached the outskirts of the city, she put the pad away and stared out the window.

She'd never lived in Montreal, but her father had, and over the years, when they'd visited, he'd shared with Gerry and her mother (when she was still alive) his favourite places and experiences. Taking the train and coming into Central Station were two of them, and Gerry always felt a pleasant anticipation mixed with nostalgia when she arrived. There were rituals to be observed. First, when they'd been a family, there was the station café to settle in for a meal: shabby, half of it little tables and chairs out in the large promenade of the station; the other half intimate booths with subdued lighting. Gerry had always preferred to sit where she could watch the business of people and luggage moving.

As a child, she'd been indulged in not having to order a sensible breakfast and had usually chosen a pastry while her parents revelled in eggs and bacon. Today, alone, she compromised by buying a take-out coffee and a sweet croissant and strolling the concourse, taking it all in.

Then, her parents had invariably visited a museum. Well, today she'd be attending a variant of that: she was going to an auction. And not at just any old auctioneer's but at Frey's, one of the oldest and most prestigious houses of its type. She felt a frisson of anticipation, left the station and walked north.

The sale, which had been postponed once already, was to include her painting by twentieth-century Quebec artist Paul-Émile Borduas. It was consigned, meaning Frey's would take a percentage of the final price the painting fetched.

She was going early to view the objects before the bidding began. She smiled as she walked up the incline that was the southern flank of Mount Royal. The first thing she'd spend the money on would be raises for Prudence and Doug.

She paused. That might be awkward. Not Prudence, but Doug. Then she shrugged. It wasn't like she was Doug's sole employer. He cut the grass and maintained the gardens and shrubs, did odd repairs on the house, but he worked at plenty of other places as well. And she had no idea if or when Aunt Maggie had last given him a raise.

After raises, she wanted to get bids from contractors to insulate The Maples. Centuries old, it was liveable in winter, as long as you avoided the edges of rooms along outside walls; and Gerry's favourite, the bamboo room where she preferred to work, was shut up completely due to its frigid temperature.

That reminded her: she'd be able to move back in there in a few weeks. Oh, happiness! Spring was just around the corner.

She stood outside Frey's. A small window — bulletproof glass, I'll bet, she thought — displayed a Chinese vase. The front of the building was grey granite blocks in which was embedded a shining brass door, studded with bolts.

She rang the bell and knew a security camera was scrutinizing her. The door opened and an armed guard let her in. He escorted her to the receptionist seated behind a round work station, centrally located in the large atrium. As the woman looked for Gerry's name on her list, Gerry allowed her gaze to travel upward to the amazing glass and lead dome. She produced I.D., signed in and was tagged, for all the world, she thought, like one of the articles up for sale.

Still, you couldn't fault their security, she concluded. She passed from the foyer, where people stood among four big palm trees, into the show room itself.

She'd received the catalogue and studied it at home, and though she didn't intend to bid on anything, it was fun to mill around in the large room with its high ceiling as though she might be a buyer, picking up small objects carefully and circling furniture. Of her painting, or any paintings, there was no sign, and she assumed they were lined up elsewhere awaiting their turn on the block.

She felt a pang for the Borduas, a small painting, a delicate abstract in black and white with hints of other colours — a little green, a little pink — subtly embedded. Perhaps Aunt Maggie had meant her to cherish it, keep it in the family. But the need for money to maintain The Maples was now. Why, she'd already depleted Aunt Maggie's $50,000 in savings left to her by almost a third and she'd only been in the house not quite a year!

She let memories of a new septic system and roof repairs dissipate, and passed into the auction room where she found a vacant chair as the auctioneer gently cleared his throat into a microphone.

She was seated between a middle-aged man — exceedingly thin, with a sniffy nose — and a very old woman wearing a turban and full-length fur coat. There was the smell of pipe tobacco from her left and one of mothballs and strong perfume from her right. Gerry's fingers itched for her sketchpad but she knew it might not be the thing to take it out and start drawing caricatures. Especially as her subjects were so close. She focused instead on the front of the room.

A small desk was elevated on a slowly rotating stand. Why, there was a similar desk in a corner of her dining room! Gerry sat up straight. She might learn something here today.

The reserve had been set at $10,000. Gerry's eyebrows rose. The man next to her began sniffing more frequently and held up a hand. The old lady looked at her rings.

The desk went for $25,000. The sniffy man gave up at $20,000. Gerry got out her sketchpad and started making notes.

The next item was a ceramic umbrella stand. There was one just like it inside The Maples' front door. Gerry's eyes bulged when it sold for $800. An *umbrella stand*?

She was so fascinated at the possibility that The Maples might have other hidden treasures, besides the Borduas, that she almost forgot her painting. Then the first art work was wheeled in and she felt the tension in the room increase.

In terms of money amounts, the furniture and most of the small objects had been warm-ups. Now it was time for the big boys and girls to play.

Gerry didn't know how she felt about the inflated prices. Even drawings by famous artists were valuable. Could a piece of art, made by the artist in hours, days or weeks, really be worth millions of dollars a few decades later? Apparently, it was, as a large Lawren Harris painting went for $1.5 million.

Neither the sniffy man nor the bejewelled old lady bid, though they followed the proceedings with interest.

As the afternoon went on, Gerry wondered when the Borduas would come out for its moment of glory. When the auctioneer banged his gavel and said, "Thank you, ladies and gentlemen, *mesdames et messieurs*, for your attendance at Frey's today," she blinked and slowly stood up.

"My painting. My painting was supposed to be sold," she said plaintively into the air. The auctioneer had already left his platform.

"What?" said the sniffy man.

"What?" said the old lady. They both turned to her.

"My Borduas. Where is it?" Gerry felt a tightness in her throat and a buzzing in her ears.

"She's going to faint," said the old lady grimly. "Go get water, Bertie," she instructed the man. "And get Adams."

Gerry felt her eyesight dim as little spots of light appeared against a dark red background. The old woman must have sat her down because when she came to, her head was between her knees.

The water when it came was cool and so was Adams. As Gerry drank, she looked up. And up. And up. Adams appeared to be about ten feet tall. It's because you're sitting down, a sensible inner voice reassured. Adams was speaking. "I am Ms. Adams, assistant to Mr. Frey. I've been looking for you, Ms. Coneybear." Adams managed to make it sound as if Gerry was somehow at fault. The old lady spoke sharply. "Never mind all that, Adams. Where's the girl's painting? A Paul-Émile, she says."

Adams soothed the old lady, or tried. "Mrs. Stewart. How nice you could attend. Are you a friend of Ms. Coneybear's?"

To Gerry's astonishment, Mrs. Stewart nodded. "Knew her grandmother. Girls together. Get on with it."

Ms. Adams seemed a bit taken aback. She addressed Gerry directly. "Perhaps my office would be a more appropriate place for this discussion, Ms. Coneybear? If you would follow me." She turned and walked away.

"Help her up, Bertie." The sniffy man did so.

"Shall we accompany you to this meeting?" he asked sympathetically.

"Did you know my grandmother too?" Gerry asked him.

"I? I know your grandmother? I, Ms. Coneybear, am neither a Coneybear nor a Stewart but a Smith, a humble antiques dealer." He presented his card. Gerry read: Edward Albert Smith, Furniture and Objets d'Arts. She looked up at him. He seemed kind.

"Yes. Yes, I think I would appreciate that." She turned to include Mrs. Stewart. "You too, please." The lady nodded grimly.

The three of them followed Ms. Adams out of the room, through the foyer, where Adams had a word with the receptionist. (And not a kind word, it seemed, as the woman shrank down at her desk.) Adams turned and said crisply, "This way, please."

They followed her austere, grey-suited form to an elevator that they took one level down. Though it was below ground, this floor was still elegantly appointed. Where there had been marble floors in the upstairs foyer, down here they were dark green linoleum. But the walls were wood-panelled and small green silk-shaded wall lamps lit their way. They stepped into Adams's office.

The room was large with wall-to-wall carpeting of a rich golden colour and cream-painted walls. Behind the desk, a light well, its bricks painted white, illuminated the room naturally. The phone rang and Ms. Adams spoke softly into it then hung up. "Excuse me. I'll have some refreshments sent in." She left the room.

"Whew!" Bertie exhaled. "I've never been in here before."

"Haven't you?" Mrs. Stewart said dourly. "It's not usually good news."

"Were you really at school with my Gramma Ellie?" Gerry asked. Someone knocked at the door then entered with a trolley. A teapot and a coffeepot were accompanied by some scones and butter. The trolley boy left.

Mrs. Stewart removed the lid off the teapot and peered inside. "Not strong enough yet. Probably only put one bag in. Yes, I knew Ellie Catford. Married Coneybear. We went to Cheaters' together."

Gerry poured herself a coffee. "Cheaters?" she asked, feeling she was in some kind of British farce. She lifted the coffee pot in Mr. Smith's direction and he nodded. She poured another cup.

"Chattos'. The Misses Chatto ran it. It's still going." Mrs. Stewart chortled. "I bet the girls still call it Cheaters." She took a scone and liberally buttered it.

"Perhaps your tea is strong enough now," Gerry suggested. Through a mouthful of scone, Mrs. Stewart nodded. She licked her fingers as Gerry poured.

"So this Borduas, how big is it?" Smith asked politely.

"About fourteen by sixteen inches." Gerry held out her hands. "This big."

The other two exchanged a look. "Small enough," Smith said.

Mrs. Stewart nodded. "Could be done," she agreed. "It's not as if they're electronically tagged — like clothes."

"What? You think my painting was stolen? From Frey's?" Gerry looked thunderstruck. At that point, Adams re-entered the room and sat behind her desk.

"Ms. Coneybear, it seems your painting, lot 351, has gone missing." Gerry sucked in her breath. The others leaned forward. Adams continued. "I have, of course, informed Mr. Frey, who was out of town at his country home, and he is driving into Montreal as we speak. We will give this matter our greatest attention."

"What's the insurance situation?" Smith asked shrewdly.

Ms. Adams swallowed. "If we cannot recover the painting, House of Frey is of course responsible as it was in our care."

Gerry relaxed. "Oh well, that's all right then."

"Wait for it," Smith growled out of the corner of his mouth.

Adams continued. "Frey is responsible for the amount we put as a starting bid — $100,000."

Gerry protested. "But the independent appraiser's estimate was that it would go from $250,000 to possibly half a million!"

Smith whistled and even Mrs. Stewart looked impressed. Adams looked uncomfortable. "I'm sorry, Ms. Coneybear, but it's not up to Frey's. The insurance company makes the rules. But I assure you, Frey's will do everything possible to recover your painting." She stood up. "Now, if you will excuse me, I must prepare for Mr. Frey's arrival."

In a daze, Gerry stood up. "Thank you, I guess." She added, rather blankly, "I have to catch a train."

She left the office with Mr. Smith and Mrs. Stewart. As they waited for the elevator, Mrs. Stewart said, "What the hell, why don't you come to my place for supper then take the later train home. We can talk about what we're going to do. Where do you live, anyway?"

"In...in Lovering," Gerry stammered, "and...and...I can't because, because — " She burst into tears. "I have to feed the cats!"

PART 2

STALK

*K*itten couldn't sleep.

Partly, it was because the girl who fed her was tossing restlessly on her pillow, murmuring about a milkman and deliveries and saying various names, none of which Kitten recognized as belonging to her extended family of cats, so therefore being of no interest to her.

And partly, it was because of the ghosts.

If Kitten had known of a word such as concatenation, she would have used it. A concatenation of ghosts.

Which was fine.

She had been aware of a kindly presence almost from the beginning; someone or thing urging her foster mother, the big marmalade cat, to bring Kitten and her four squirming, blind brothers and sisters to the safety of The Maples.

And then months later that presence had brought her own mother to the fireplace room and sat her down in a rocking chair while she looked for something in the kitchen.

Even that hadn't bothered Kitten. The other cats hardly opened their eyes when that benevolent spirit wafted through the house. But when she brought her cat...

She was a strange one, her three-colour coat faded and tattered, her body a skeleton covered in fur. When she prowled the room grew cold. She seemed enraged. Kitten kept well away from her...

But even the negative space created by the calico cat would have been bearable; it was more than balanced by that created by the tall kindly wraith and her comfortable, complaining little mother.

No. Kitten couldn't sleep because she sensed a shift, a turning of some great wheel, an opening through which others were beginning to stream.

Why, look at those two in the corner of the bedroom — a tall dark man and a small pretty woman — clasping hands and leaning close, smiling and talking in low voices together.

Harmless, you would have thought. Yet, when the girl in the bed finally got up and carried Kitten downstairs, they followed close behind them, looking into Kitten's frightened eyes as she peered over the girl's shoulder, and when the girl was making tea in the kitchen, the man flicked a wrist to make a portrait of a middle-aged man fall from the foyer wall. Then, after the girl had run in and leaned it against the wall and turned away, the woman likewise caused it to tip forward.

The two then laughed, a bit hysterically, Kitten thought. She returned to the dining room where two more ghosts sat at the massive table. One of them was horrible.

He seemed to be an older man and he was horrible because of his head. Sometimes his face was visible, and you could see where it had been a kind face though now filled with sorrow. But sometimes this face peeled away until just the raw meat and bone remained, like the insides of a mouse, freshly eviscerated. He had one of the big black and white cats on his lap. He said to his companion, a very old, very fat woman with dark laughing eyes, "Cats are so comforting, aren't they?" She had the other big cat on her lap and nodded.

And behind him stood another dark-eyed, dark-haired man and behind the woman stood a pale man, with one hand on her shoulder, as though they were posed for a formal photograph.

The big black and white cats blinked gravely at Kitten from the ghastly man's lap and from the fat woman's, as if to say, "This is how to welcome friendly spirits."

Kitten knew they were right. The four apparitions in the dining room, the young couple still in the foyer, the two women in the living room rocking chairs, weren't there to hurt anyone, least of all a little black cat with white legs, but she sensed, beyond them, lurking at the edges, were other beings who were not so benevolent.

6

Gerry sifted the dry ingredients then slowly added them to the already whisked wet. She was making one of Aunt Maggie's recipes — Jumbo Ginger Cookies with Buttercream Icing — for the first time. "Six per pan" someone had written at the top of the little stained piece of paper, cut out from a magazine long ago. "Makes sense," Gerry commented to Jay, who, from behind the sink taps, was watching these preparations, reaching out a tentative paw when water dripped from the faucet. "They are supposed to be jumbo."

Jay seemed the same since her operation. Gerry had worried that the kitten, plunged suddenly into middle age, would lose interest in play, would gain weight. She smiled. Bea wouldn't like that description of midlife. Her friend, in her fifties, and living life mostly from a wheelchair, enjoyed herself; was involved in almost every facet of Lovering's social life.

Gerry popped a pan of cookies into the oven and ran a little water to do the dishes. Jay put out a paw, drawing the stream of water towards her. She licked her wet claws and continued studying the faucet. "Seen any more ghosts, Jay?" Gerry teased. The cat looked at a point on the floor between the kitchen's back door and the fridge, as if indicating, Gerry suddenly thought with a shiver, "There's one right there."

Jay jumped down from the counter and pounced on a ladybug. Gerry laughed. She took the first pan of cookies out of the oven and admired. The spicy batter had spread and puffed.

"These *are* jumbo." She put the second pan into the oven and went to tidy the living room.

As she moved chairs around and dusted, she thought about the mysterious loss of her painting.

When she had returned home the day of the auction, there had been a long message from Mr. Frey in which he asked her to be discreet and not tell anyone about the fiasco at his business. "Please," he'd begged. "Just give us a few days to make an internal investigation, and I'm sure we can clear this up."

She'd phoned her own insurance company, only to be informed of what she'd suspected: when she'd physically consigned the Borduas to Frey's, Frey's insurance had taken the place of hers.

She shrugged her shoulders, pushed the sofa so it was farther from the fire up against the wall, and moved the rocking chairs to the far end of the living room, substituting a half dozen straight-backed chairs. She still had money in the bank, and the insurance company would reimburse her, if partially, if the Borduas wasn't recovered.

She sighed. How dignified House of Frey's ad had seemed when she'd seen it in the paper months ago. "Invitation To Consign" it had said at the top, and "Please contact us for complimentary and confidential valuations."

"You shouldn't believe everything you read," she muttered and sighed again. It was out of her control. All she could do today was give her art students a good experience. She ticked them off on her fingers.

Judith, Christine and Ben were from the first group she'd taught last fall; June and Sharon from the second, winter class. Five was a nice number for a sketching class.

She finished baking the cookies and set them to cool. She decided to clean the back porch.

Accessed through the rear of the main entranceway, the square screened back porch was one of Gerry's favourite parts of

The Maples. In winter, when it was just a firewood storage facility, she didn't think about it, but this fine April day, with sounds of meltwater dripping and courting birds twittering, sweeping it became a symbol of spring, an opening up of the world.

She folded the big tarp covering the floor and took it outside to shake. Then she swept the remaining bits of bark and wood chips into a central pile and disposed of them. She vacuumed and washed the porch floor and wished she didn't have the class to teach. Wouldn't it be wonderful to sit out here and relax? Tomorrow, she promised herself, and went inside to ice the cookies. She had to test one to make sure they were okay. Big and soft and fragrant with spices, topped with a thick swirl of buttercream, they were so good, she had another. So much for lunch.

She had the students draw from memory that day. "It could be a face, a landscape, a room," Gerry suggested. "It could be one little thing, like an ornament you remember, or something you dreamt. See what happens when you have to rely on your inner eye."

As usual, Sharon, whose forehead was wrinkled in a permanent frown, drew slowly, with heavy thick lines. Judith, Christine and June were pretty good, while Ben fell somewhere in between. Gerry found herself drawing her mother's face, similar to her own, but with a serenity Gerry felt she herself lacked. When she was satisfied, she went to make tea.

Upon her return with refreshments, she asked each person to exhibit and describe their memory. Sharon had found a subject worthy of her strong style. "It's the old sawmill. Used to be just before Dead Man's Corner. I grew up hearing the whine of the saws."

Judith, a gentle twenty-something, had also tried a building, that housing the *Lovering Herald*, where she worked with her father. Her soft shading showed her affection for the place.

Christine, an elegant senior, had, predictably, drawn her garden. "I could probably do it in my sleep," she laughed. And Ben, also a senior, short and trim, had drawn his smart car and given it a face. "Well, I feel it's alive," he explained as the women laughed and admired.

June — small, plump, fortyish — showed her drawing last. Gerry, who knew June had difficulty speaking in public, prompted her. "It looks like a group of people standing on a lawn." June nodded and Gerry looked more closely. "Why, June, it looks like *my* back lawn." June nodded again. "Were you ever here for a function?" June shook her head. "So this isn't a memory then?" June shook then hung her head as if ashamed. "Never mind," Gerry encouraged. "Next time — "

"I see them," June whispered, pointing toward the backyard through the window. "Standing."

"You've left out the faces," Sharon said briskly.

For some reason, Gerry felt a prickle of fear somewhere at the back of her neck. "Must be your memory of a photo in the *Lovering Herald*. One of Maggie's committee meetings perhaps, or a garden party?"

Christine looked more closely. "No. These women are dressed old-fashioned. Look at those flat hats." She straightened her seventy-something back. "Before my time."

June, embarrassed by the attention, took another cookie. Gerry consulted the time. "Well, I think that's enough for today. If any of you want to finish your sketches and show us them next class, that might be fun."

As June left, shepherded into a car by her solicitous husband, she whispered to Gerry, "Sorry."

Gerry, feeling drained by the day's efforts, moved the living room furniture back into place, fed the cats and went for a nap. She woke up when someone rang the doorbell. It was Doug and he had falafel.

"You are the best boyfriend ever!" she said as she threw her arms around him.

"The way to your heart is, I know, take-out," he grinned. They unpacked the feast at the living room table. Cats, attracted by savoury odours, gathered.

"Falafel sandwiches. And chicken sandwiches. And roasted potatoes with garlic mayo! Now I can die and go to heaven," Gerry said happily.

"Don't say such things," he muttered and drew her to him. "It feels funny to be called a boyfriend at my age."

And Gerry, who rarely compared Doug's forty-three years to her own twenty-six, and already knew he was sensitive about the difference, hugged him and kept silent.

As they dug into the feast, the cats kept a respectful distance. All except Jay, who, excited by first the art class and now Doug's presence, let her manners go out the window and crowded them while they ate. Gerry held out a finger with a drop of hot sauce on it. Jay recoiled and retreated to the table's edge where she sneezed, giving them reproachful glances.

"Sorry, Jay, but everybody gets the same treatment. No human food for cats." Bob, sitting nearby, knew differently, as being Gerry's favourite he was sometimes spoiled with a bit of tuna, chicken or beef, but secretly. He smirked.

Doug took a sip of water. "So, how was the class?"

"Good. I think." Gerry's brow wrinkled. "I think one of the students may have thought she had a vision or something." She described June's sketch and her own explanation of it.

"I'm with you," Doug concluded. "It does sound like June sketched a group photograph."

Gerry shrugged. "Never mind that, I have to tell you what happened at the auction yesterday."

When she'd finished, Doug sat straight up. "And how reputable is this company?"

"House of Frey? Well, they've been in business since the 1920s. I met two interesting people there too." She went on to describe Mrs. Stewart and Bertie Smith.

"Sound like a couple of characters," Doug offered.

"They are. And they were immediately suspicious that the painting could have been stolen, not mislaid."

"Why?" He helped himself to his second sandwich and pushed the potatoes with mayo towards Gerry.

"Well, they thought the fact that the painting is a small one would make it easy to take. And the fact that there's such a discrepancy between the insurance assessment and sale price. Someone who had a private buyer could make a bundle. And all that would happen would be Frey's insurance premium would go up."

Doug whistled. "Wow. Nice work if you can get it. But risky for the thief, no?"

Gerry nodded. "Terribly. If they're a Frey employee." She started stuffing garbage into a paper bag. "Mr. Frey asked for my discretion for a few days so don't tell anyone else, okay?"

"Okay."

"How's the cigarette reduction project going?"

He groaned. "Don't remind me of cigarettes. It makes me want one. I've had four already today. I'm going to have one more when I get home tonight."

"That's good, isn't it? You were at eight a day last week, I think."

"Yes. Eight. Or nine." He seemed to be thinking about something else.

"Where are the boys?"

"Over at Mary's." His face set grimly. "Margaret got out yesterday and they're having a reunion."

"Oh, God," Gerry said faintly.

"You can imagine how this is going to affect the boys. I'm going to pick them up at nine-thirty."

Gerry put her hand in his. "How about some TLC before you have to go." Together, they went upstairs and closed her bedroom door.

7

Prudence savoured an after-lunch jumbo ginger cookie. "Not bad. I remember Maggie used to tint the icing orange and make them look like jack o'lanterns around Halloween."

"Remind me to do that next fall," Gerry said absently. She finished the dedication and signed the inside front cover of her book. "And don't even think of paying me," she said. "You helped with the cake research, remember?"

Prudence received her copy of *The Cake-Jumping Cats of Dibble*. "Thank you," she said, turning the pages. "Ah, yes, the Battenberg cake." She closed the book. "I have a favour to ask." Gerry looked up from admiring her book. "Is it too last minute to ask you to drive me to the penitentiary today? This afternoon?"

Gerry thought quickly. "Where is it?"

"North. About an hour's drive. I'll drive, if you like. And pay for the gas. Just — I feel I need the company."

Gerry regretfully let go of her idea of a few hours on the back porch and pushed all worries about *Mug the Bug* deadlines and book marketing aside. There was always the evening in which to work. She could do with a break from her daily routine. "Okay. It's good timing, 'cause I've got to take Harley and Kitty-Cat to the vet tomorrow, and Saturday is the CRAS event. I'm ready when you are."

They took the highway northwest of Lovering, crossed the Ottawa River and headed back east. "It's a roundabout route," Prudence acknowledged, "but it's better than driving into Montreal and then going northwest. No traffic."

Gerry chatted lightly about mutual acquaintances, wondering if there would be a get-together with Markie Stribling when she arrived for her next visit to Lovering. "I thought she was coming for Easter, but that's in three days so maybe I was mistaken."

Prudence grunted.

Gerry switched topics. "I don't know. It seems the cats are edgy. Like something's going to happen."

Prudence suggested, "Picking up on your missing painting? Margaret coming home?

"Yee-es. Maybe the latter. But I think it started before I knew she was getting out of the institution."

"Speaking of which," Prudence said drily, turning off the road and approaching a guardhouse, "we're here."

The prison looked more like a factory than anything else — a big grey windowless block stuck in a field. They were directed to a more friendly-looking administrative building adjacent to the block.

"My cousin," Prudence explained, as they signed in, and Gerry felt the glow of kinship.

They walked to a visiting area and were seated one side of a thick glass window. Gerry peered around nervously. "I thought they had rooms with tables for visiting," she whispered.

"Television," Prudence muttered. "This is an old facility. Maximum security. They frown on bank robbers and murderers in Quebec." She straightened up as the door the other side of the glass opened and a guard sat Alexander Crick down.

He had a handsome face, still unlined, which Gerry thought odd in a man who must be almost sixty. A straight nose, full lips and a strong jaw added to his appearance. The only unattractive touch was the buzz cut. And the eyes.

They were clear, unconcerned. Gerry had expected to see pain, guilt, furtiveness — any number of negative emotions. But the expression was bland. She turned her attention to Prudence.

In her face were expressed all those negative emotions, as well as anger and fear, and Prudence looked suddenly like an old woman. Gerry put out a hand and clasped her friend's.

"And who's this?" Alexander asked, pleasantly enough.

"Gerry Coneybear's girl. Also called Gerry."

"Gerald Coneybear. The one who got away," mused Alexander.

Prudence flushed. Gerry waited for a further discussion of her father but none came. Had Prudence had a crush on her dad?

"How's your mother, Prudence?"

Prudence started. "If you must know, she's dead. More than ten years ago. What do you want?"

He paused a moment, looking at her. "I'm sorry. For you, anyway. I know she was your best friend. I didn't know she'd died. I don't get many visitors." He paused again. "They're letting me go," he added, the look in his eyes before he lowered them becoming dazed. "After all these years."

"When?" Prudence's voice sounded hard.

"Next week." He looked up. "Oh, don't worry. I'm not going to impose on you. I'll be staying at The Mountainview. At first."

"Well. Good." Prudence sounded and looked relieved. Gerry felt her hand relax. "And then?"

"I don't know. Stay at the farm for a while. Probably move away. Start over. At fifty-eight." He laughed sadly. "Just thought I'd tell you. In case we bump into each other."

"I'm hardly going to bump into you at The Mountainview, am I?" Prudence said drily, almost with an attempt at humour.

He took it as such and laughed. "No. I guess not." And added, as Prudence rose suddenly, "Thanks for coming, Prue. I wish — "

Prudence flushed again and they left. So there was someone who called Prudence by a nickname! Gerry wondered if Aunt Maggie had also called her Prue. "I'll drive," she offered.

Gerry reflected that the visit had been oddly brief considering its two main actors hadn't seen each other for twenty-five years, but she didn't probe Prudence. Instead, when they were back on the southbound highway headed to home, Gerry asked, "What's The Mountainview?"

"Strip club and cheap motel. On the old highway. Just past that nice greenhouse where we bought the annuals last year."

"So, nowhere near Lovering," Gerry offered.

"Near enough," was the gruff response. Then Prudence added, "He used to have red hair. Long red hair." No more was said as Gerry sensed Prudence was in some pain.

Gerry drove right to Prudence's house. She thought her friend looked weary as she walked to the front door of her cute little white cottage with its gabled porch. Gone were its Christmas decorations. Instead, Prudence had stuck stiff red artificial tulips in her window boxes. The effect was quirky. Gerry called out the car window, "Nice!" gesturing at the display. Prudence managed a weak smile and a wave.

At Gerry's, it was, of course, feeding time at the zoo. In fact, it was past feeding time, so the usually nonchalant cats rushed to greet her when she let herself in. "I know! I know!" she exclaimed, shooing them from the kitchen so she could prepare their nineteen individual plates in peace. "Don't blame me! Blame Alexander Crick!"

The first thing Gerry did next morning — well, the first thing after chores and while she was drinking her coffee — was to phone her publisher. "By Tuesday? That's great! Yeah, another hundred. Okay. Thanks." If she dropped off books at all the places she planned to over the next few days, she'd run out of copies. Assuming she sold a few at the cat adoption event. "Fingers crossed, Bob," she cooed at the cat on her work table. Bob, who had already crossed his front paws one over the other, blinked encouragement. He seemed to have every confidence in her.

Her next call was to one of her friends, a close neighbour, Cathy Stribling of Fieldcrest B&B. "Cathy, Gerry. Any plans for the weekend?"

Cathy sounded harassed. "Oh, Gerry, I'm doing laundry. Going to have a full house of customers this weekend. And Markie's flying in tonight. Andrew's going to get her and she'll be staying at his place. I'm kind of stuck here when I have clients. Perhaps Andrew will have an Easter dinner?"

Gerry felt disappointed. She'd envisioned a big Easter feast with her friends. "Not that I've heard. I guess he'll want to be with Markie. I feel like I'm too busy to see people and then when I try, they're too busy."

"It's winter, too," her friend replied. "Just ending. And so long. We've all been pretty hunkered down."

"Yeah. I guess. Oh, Cathy, I met Alexander Crick yesterday."

"What!?" She had Cathy's attention now. "What!? Prudence's husband? I remember him! He was handsome. Where? Where did you meet him?"

"In prison. But he's getting out in a few days. He wanted to tell Prudence. Warn her, I guess, so she wouldn't be shocked if she saw him around."

"Gerry, I just — you take my breath away! I thought he was in for life!"

"Is he a killer, Cathy?" Gerry asked in a small voice.

"That's just it! We don't know. There was a bank robbery. They were all armed. And one of them whacked a guard over the head with an iron paperweight on someone's desk inside the bank. And as they all wore masks and kept silent during the robbery, the bank employees couldn't identify who did it. Alex was the only one to get caught and for some reason, wasn't willing to point a finger at the guilty one. But he didn't confess or deny it either. Strange, eh? So he got the maximum sentence."

"He was afraid of him, I suppose. The killer," Gerry said slowly. "If he had connections…"

"Right. So that means the guard's death probably wasn't Alexander's doing as he doesn't have any. Connections, criminal or otherwise. Apart from Prudence. His family turned their backs on him long before the robbery."

"Huh. So Alexander didn't do it but may know who did."

"And another thing, Gerry. They got away and it was weeks before Alex got caught. The money was never found. They hid it, I suppose." A long drawn-out baying could be heard at Cathy's end. "Prince Charles wants his walk, Gerry. Gotta go!"

Which reminded Gerry: she had two pet-related duties to accomplish. She dressed and loaded Harley and Kitty-Cat one each in the two cat carriers and drove to the vet, credit card in hand, and with a few more copies of *The Cake-Jumping Cats of Dibble* — just in case.

She was glad she did as all the copies she'd dropped off the previous Saturday had sold. "Oh, good, you brought more!" the receptionist said happily. "Now I can buy one. It's funny! I read it but they sold out so quickly, I didn't get my own copy. I mention them and point out that they're to benefit CRAS whenever someone pays."

Gerry thanked her, and sat down to wait. Friday wasn't as busy at the vets as Saturday had been, and she was soon seen by Dr. Morin this time.

As usual, the vet made Gerry feel a frump, with her elegant coiffure and manicured nails, nylons and high heels. But she was swift and gentle with the "Big Boys" as she called them. There was no need for a vet tech to strong-arm the two placid cats.

"Nothing the matter here," she concluded, scattering cat candy on the table in front of Harley. "They just need their shots and some flea repellent and they're good to go." She washed her hands as Gerry gently stuffed the cats back into their carriers. "I read your little book. You're very talented." Gerry smiled. "Would you take on a commission for me?" Gerry nodded. "My partner has an old dog. A very old dog. And I thought it would be nice if he had a painting of the dog—to remember it by." Gerry enthusiastically agreed. "All right. I'll leave some photos with the receptionist and you can pick them up some time."

Though her credit card had had a workout, Gerry left the vet's considerably more cheered than she had been when she'd gone in. A $500 commission! That would pay for three and a half cats to have their checkups! Plus, every time she sold thirty books, she made $150, which equalled another cat's medical expenses.

"It's working, cats," she said to Harley and Kitty-Cat on the drive home. "It's working." As she drove past Doug's driveway, she felt the urge to see him but reasoned he must be out at one job or another. And she had the cats. "You guys okay if I just grab a few things?" They seemed the opposite of anxious so she popped into Lovering's grocery store, the list of essentials in her pocket.

She hummed as she zoomed around the store, mindful of the two waiting in the car. She was just heaving a box of cat litter into her cart (always left to the end—who wanted to push those thirty pounds around?) when two female figures hesitated at the end of the pet supplies aisle before moving on.

Had that been—? Could it be—? Gerry pushed her cart in the figures' direction, paused at the end of the aisle and looked either way. Two women in high heels, designer raincoats and with carefully dressed hair were just turning into the fruit and vegetable section. She caught a glimpse of their profiles. It was Aunt Mary and Cousin Margaret.

"Argh!" Gerry muttered. "Not today! Not today, ladies!" She turned and raced back down the pet aisle, turned right and rushed to a cashier that was free.

"Hi, Gerry," said the tall bagboy.

"David." Gerry looked blankly at Doug and Margaret's youngest son. Unlike his older brothers James and Geoff Jr., David liked Gerry. "I didn't know you work here." Hurry up, hurry up, she urged the young cashier silently.

David packed her supplies slowly. "Dad said I could work here part-time during school and full-time in the summer. I want to earn enough money to pay for school myself. And maybe take a trip."

"Well, good for you." Gerry helped him pack then fumbled with her wallet.

"Did ya see Mum and Gramma Mary? They just got here. Mum looks great." David looked so happy that Gerry's heart sank. Oh, how she wished it was true and Margaret was better. If only for her sons' sakes. But how could she be? She looked furtively around.

Gerry saw Mary. Mary saw Gerry. She put out a hand to halt the progress of her cart, being pushed by Margaret. "You're doing a great job, David," the proud grandmother said loudly. The boy flushed with pleasure. Margaret looked stonily past Gerry toward her son. "Great job, David," she echoed tonelessly. Mary pulled on the cart and Margaret resumed pushing. They turned down the cookie aisle.

"Gramma Mary loves her sweets," David chatted. "You want me to push your cart outside, Gerry?"

Gerry nodded. At the car, as David unloaded her stuff, she asked, "Does your mum seem better, David?"

He straightened. "Well, at least she's talking now. Last fall, when Grampa Geoff died—" The boy's voice trembled. "She just stopped talking. And eating."

Self-punishment, Gerry thought gloomily. She handed David a two-dollar coin. "Thanks, David. And I hope she keeps getting better and better." Her tone changed to one of fondness. "Look at those two, asleep in their boxes." She indicated Harley and Kitty-Cat.

"I love cats," David confessed. "They're so self-composed."

"Have you met my cat Lightning?" Gerry asked. "She's far from self-composed. But then something really bad happened to her once." Like to your mother, she added, but didn't say the words aloud.

At home, unpacking her groceries, Gerry decided she needed a bit of normalcy. She phoned her closest neighbour, Blaise Parminter, and invited herself to tea.

A retired English professor and published poet, Blaise was in his nineties. He lived with two cats: Graymalkin, who had formerly lived at The Maples; and Ariel, a stray, and the mother of the five kittens, including Jay, Gerry had fostered last autumn.

All three met Gerry at the front door of Blaise's Victorian monstrosity around three that afternoon. "Are you enjoying these longer lighter afternoons as much as I am?" he asked as they sat down in the living room by a gas fire.

"Of course," she replied, picking Ariel up. "This one looks fatter." The little cat, black with white legs, settled on Gerry's lap and began a robust purr. She'd been feral and near death when Graymalkin rescued her and brought her home on a cold night that winter.

"She does enjoy her meat," Blaise stated. He bent to caress the sleek grey male cat sitting at his feet. "But I always save the best for Graymalkin here." The big cat's green eyes flashed in the light as he curved his head backwards towards his owner. "I'll never forget coming into the kitchen one morning last winter and seeing not one but two cats tucking into the leftover beef Wellington from your birthday party."

"And then you phoned me to come and take Ariel to the vet for a checkup." Gerry didn't add that that had been the morning after Doug had first slept over, and Blaise's call had interrupted some, er, interesting activity. She teased, "Soon you'll have a dozen cats running around here, Blaise."

"No. Two is enough for me."

They chatted by the fire. Gerry produced a copy of her cat book for Blaise, which he promptly asked her to read aloud. He laughed in all the right places. Then Gerry made the tea and set it before them. Blaise had instructed her to open a package of gingersnaps to crunch or dip as they fancied. The cats edged closer, hoping for crumbs. "What are you doing for Easter, Blaise?"

"My nephew is picking me up on Sunday and bringing me to his place for a meal. I hope it doesn't rain. There's nothing drearier than being a passenger in a car being driven on a rainy day. I won't sleep there but I will be late. Could you pop in around this time and give these two their suppers?"

"I don't see why not," Gerry said. "I've no particular plans. Blaise, do you, or did you know Prudence's husband, Alexander Crick?"

"Ah." Blaise leaned back and a tired look came to his face. "A sad story. The bad boy."

"The bad boy?" Gerry wondered why that phrase had a familiar ring to it.

"Oh, you know. Every class has one, usually. Some are worse than others. I always thought Alex's badness had a questioning quality about it."

"Questioning?"

"Yes. Like when a cat sits on the counter pushing a pencil or something closer and closer to the edge, all the while looking at you to see how you're going to react."

"My cats would never play such tricks on me," Gerry said primly, looking at Graymalkin, with whom she'd always had a difficult relationship.

"Huh. I'll bet. Not him. Her." Ariel blinked innocently and jumped back up on Gerry's lap.

"Her? Never!" she joked.

"She's still very young. Not quite a year, the vet says. She likes to play." He paused. "What were we talking about?"

"Alex Crick. Being a bad boy."

"Yes. Always pushing, testing. As if to say 'Will you still love me if I do this?' And of course, it wore one down."

"His family? Prudence?"

"Yes. And his teachers and classmates, though the young don't take bad behaviour as seriously as adults do. I remember one episode in which Alex and another boy hung a smaller boy out of a third-floor window at school."

"What!?"

"Yes. By holding on to his legs. And when asked if he understood how serious the situation might have become, Alex said that if, for whatever reason, one of them had let go, the other would have been strong enough to hold on."

"Strange logic," Gerry said slowly.

"Yes. He came from a large family. One of twelve, I believe. Of course they'd have been born in the 1920s, '30s, and '40s. It was still common back then."

"And he got lost among so many," Gerry, the single child, mused. "And then he met Prudence."

"I assume they just grew up together. You'd have to ask her how they became a couple."

"One doesn't ask Prudence intimate stuff like that, I've learned."

"No. A very private person was how Maggie once described her." He closed his eyes.

Gerry removed and washed the tea things before calling a gentle goodbye and walking pensively home. As she turned her key in the lock, she realized why Blaise's words "the bad boy" had resonated with her.

8

The bad boy is 13 years old. The bad boy doesn't live in Lovering but almost in the next village, far away down the river road. The bad boy lives on a farm with 11 brothers and sisters. The bad boy wears rubber boots to school all year. The bad boy has failed grade six twice. Once more and he will be only one grade above me and my friend Prudence Catford. We are in grade four. Last year I won a general proficiency prize. I won in grades one and two as well. My name is Maggie Coneybear.

Very pleased with herself, thought Gerry about the writer, and felt a twinge of pity for the bad boy.

The bad boy brings sugar and lard sandwiches to school. He says they taste delicious but Prue and I think they look disgusting.

The bad boy will do anything on a dare. This winter he stuck his tongue on the monkey bars in the school playground. Everyone stood around and watched as Mrs. Young poured warm water on his tongue. Just as she began to pour, the bad boy wrenched his tongue off the metal and stuck it out, all bloody, at us girls. It looked nasty. Mrs. Young made him rinse his mouth out with salt water so he wouldn't get an infection. And she sent a note home to his parents. On the bus, the bad boy laughed and tore the note up. "My parents can't read," he said, and threw the bits out the bus window. Which makes him a litterbug, Prue says. I like that word — litterbug. It makes me think of ladybugs. "Ladybug, ladybug, fly away home. Your house is on fire and your children all gone." I think the ladybug must be Alexander Crick's mother.

Gerry was beginning to recognize her aunt's juvenile style. Though this was more of a personal essay than "The Singing Milkman" had been, and lacked its charm, it shared a similar abrupt ending. And she noticed that here was another person who had called Prudence Prue.

She stretched. Gingersnaps and tea were all very well, but they hadn't filled her up. Supper? Why not. She went to stand in front of the open fridge. As usual, she was not inspired.

What would Prudence do? Oh, she'd make pastry and a cream sauce, fry meat and chop vegetables, and serve herself a delicious chicken pot pie, the inner Gerry ruminated. I've made fruit pies. Why not a supper pie? She checked the clock. Five. How long does a meaty pie take? She checked one of Aunt Maggie's basic cookbooks — the one with the red and white plaid cover.

Not long, but they were starting with ready-made pastry and cooked chicken. And the recipe called for chicken broth, which she didn't have. It was doable. It might be an adventure, she thought doubtfully, and was saved by a bell. The phone.

"Gerry, Andrew here. How are you fixed for supper?"

"Not at all," she said cheerfully, closing the book with a snap. "What did you have in mind?"

Ten minutes later they were speeding to the airport to pick up Markie Stribling. In the car Andrew explained how they wanted to organize a nice birthday lunch for Cathy, Markie's sister, on Easter Monday. "Her guests will have checked out and she'll be pooped. Markie will be staying at my place and she'll ask her over for lunch at one. As Cathy's such a fine caterer, we need all the help we can get planning and executing this meal."

"Oh, fun, Andrew. I'm just in the mood for an afternoon with friends. Do you want me to invite people?"

"That would be huge, Gerry. Thanks. Fingers crossed they'll have had their family dos on Sunday and be free. And can some of them park at your place? So it's a surprise?"

"Of course. I'll mention it when I phone. I think Blaise will be free. What's on the menu?"

"Let's wait and discuss it over dinner. Markie will know Cathy's favourites."

When they got to the airport, Andrew pulled over and checked his phone. "She's just in there. By the doughnut shop." He released the trunk lock and jumped out of the car as Markie's tall form came through sliding doors. He kissed her on the cheek, loaded her luggage and they were off.

Markie leaned forward from the back seat and squeezed Gerry's shoulder with a large beringed hand. "Gerry! Great to see you!" She laid her other hand lightly on Andrew's shoulder and kept it there.

A little embarrassed, Gerry turned away. "Lovely to see you too, Markie. Welcome to spring in Quebec." A few snowflakes fell out of a dull grey sky.

Markie laughed. "They'll be playing golf where I live."

"I thought we'd go to the Star for supper," Andrew suggested.

"Mmm," both women expressed their approval.

"Poppadums," said Gerry.

"Pakoras," added Markie.

"Samosas," finished Andrew.

Markie caught sight of herself in the rear-view mirror. "God, I need a shave," she moaned, rubbing her face.

"I thought of that," Andrew said triumphantly. "Gerry, look in the glove compartment." Gerry found and handed Markie an electric razor.

As a buzzing came from the back seat, Markie sighed contentedly. "Love is a man with a fully-charged shaver." Andrew smiled in the mirror at her. Gerry giggled.

Markie heard her and paused. "What?"

Gerry half-turned to face her. "You two remind me of Cece and Bea. How easy you are with each other."

"That's how you know it's real," Andrew said quietly. Gerry thought of her and Doug. Was it easy between them?

At the restaurant over their appetizers, they discussed Monday's lunch.

"Ham, definitely ham," Markie said. "It's her favourite and I know the family recipe for glazing it. And scalloped potatoes. Again, I know our mother's recipe. With cheddar cheese. I better make those too."

"But what does that leave for the rest of us to bring?" Gerry asked.

"Party snacks, crudités, cheese, et cetera, for before the meal."

"I'll get some champagne and we'll have mimosas," Andrew suggested.

Markie continued. "Vegetable sides, dessert, wine with the meal, dessert. Did I mention dessert?"

Andrew smiled. "Only three times."

"I could do dessert," Gerry suggested, though she had no idea what she might make.

"Excellent," said Markie. "I hear from Cathy you're quite the baker. I'm more of a meat and potatoes ma — " She stopped herself and laughed. "The old clichés still pop out."

"So you're an aeronautics engineer *and* a brilliant chef? No fair!" complained Gerry. "I wish I could get the hang of suppers. It's just, by the time I think of it, I'm already hungry. I have been baking bread, though. Prudence just introduced me to yeast."

"There are loads of sweet Easter breads," Markie suggested.

"Oo, I don't know. I've just started. A cake is probably safer."

"Well, no pressure," Markie assured her. "Just make sure it's delicious."

While they ate their main courses, Gerry realized that the restaurant wasn't the right venue for talking to Andrew about Margaret. Not with Markie present. Once again, she wondered how much Andrew knew about his sister's involvement in Aunt Maggie's death, how Margaret had been driven to murder out of disappointment that neither her mother, Mary, nor she, Margaret, had inherited Maggie's possessions, including The Maples. And that Mary, probably without meaning to, had goaded Margaret until she snapped. No. Definitely not to be talked about with Markie there. Rats, she told herself, she should have brought it up in the car on the way to the airport. She must really, really not want to discuss it.

After masala chai and gulab jamun, they returned to their respective houses. Gerry gave the cats some attention while looking through cookbooks. After perusing recipes for braids and twists and rings, she realized she'd have to get up at four a.m. in order to have a yeasted dessert ready for lunchtime Monday.

"But I could make dinner rolls tomorrow and put them in a plastic bag to keep fresh," she announced to Bob, Mother and Jay, who were keeping her company by the cold hearth. "Nope, I forgot I'm at the cat event tomorrow. Making the cake on Sunday will be enough. So, no rolls." She turned to another book to look at the cakes.

This was one of Aunt Maggie's older books and one that Gerry had previously raided for ideas to put in *The Cake-Jumping Cats of Dibble*. First she turned to the novelty cakes section at the back of the book and was enthralled by recipes for a merry-go-round cake and an igloo cake. The child in her exulted in the fanciful shapes and decorations, and she'd almost settled on making the bunny cake, complete with ears — it was Easter, wasn't it? — when she remembered it was Cathy's birthday party.

The Easter day gateau then — a large square orange-flavoured cake layered with whipped cream and topped with marzipan oranges. The sides had sliced almonds pressed on. She sketched an alternative decoration for the top: a coconut nest with little yellow marzipan chicks. "So a birthday cake but with an Eastery flavour," she muttered. "Fun." She made a special-ingredients grocery list and went to bed.

An ear-splitting yowl jerked her from sleep. "What the — ?" She saw Bob and Lightning looking startled. But no Jay. Gerry rushed downstairs, flicking on lights as she went. The yowl was repeated.

She passed through the dining room where just-roused cats stretched and yawned. Everybody seemed to be there. Except Jay. She found her in the living room.

The kitten was going bonkers.

She bounced from chair to table to windowsill, took one look out towards the lake, ricocheted back onto the table then chair then floor, and cowered under the table. She didn't seem to notice a stupefied Gerry standing in the doorway, watching.

Suddenly, Jay ran to the front of the house, leapt onto the bench and stretched her paws to peer out the bottom of one window. "Jay, whatever — " Gerry began. She saw the kitten's head jerk up and then the little creature was climbing the curtains.

Gerry had had enough. She removed Jay, claw by claw, from the curtain material and held her firmly to her breast. Through the window, she saw a car slow, then speed up and drive on.

Jay vibrated against her, normal cat shivers alternating with violent ripples that ran from her ears to her tail. "Are you having a fit?" an aghast Gerry asked. "Do you need to see the vet?"

She carried the cat into the kitchen where the stove-top clock was displaying one of those weird times — 12:34 — that always gave her pause. She wrapped Jay in a terry tea towel and tucked her inside her robe. With one hand she poured milk into a little pot and heated it gently. Back in the living room, sitting at the table and fending off the other cats sniffing the warm milk, she offered it to Jay on the tip of her pinkie.

Slowly, the kitten became aware of the sweet-smelling treat. Slowly, she calmed down and began licking it off Gerry's finger. When she'd had enough, Gerry put the pot on the floor for the others.

Most of them sniffed it and backed away — few adult cats care for milk — but little Ronald and, surprisingly, old fat Min Min shared the liquid. Lightning looked as if she'd have liked some but lacked the confidence to fight for it.

Once the excitement was over, most of the cats drifted away and back to sleep. Gerry sat for a little while with the kitten cuddled close, its nose in the crook of her elbow, and wondered what could have caused the uproar.

From the kitchen came a faint clank. She listened. Metal on metal. There was a screeching sound of pans and pots crashing together.

Gerry rushed to look. One lower kitchen cupboard door was slightly ajar. Jay jumped down and pushed her head inside. Gerry bent down and fully opened the door.

A collection of cookie sheets and cupcake pans cascaded onto the kitchen floor. Gerry picked up a loaf pan. Little black ovals were deposited in one corner of the pan. Jay rooted around in the cupboard for a while, then poked her head out, looking up at Gerry. Disgusted that such a small thing had caused all the commotion, Gerry said one word, "Mice!" and added traps to her shopping list.

9

A bleary-eyed Gerry scrambled out of bed at seven Saturday morning. She made her breakfast and prepared for the cat adoption event, deciding jeans with a nice shirt and sweater would be perfectly appropriate. She made sure she had a pen with which to sign copies, and put some books in a plastic bag then into a small box.

Outside, a fine drizzle melted the snow, and she was thrilled to see patches of lawn appearing. She wiped the condensation from the window and looked closer. Yes! Clumps of little white snowdrops were in flower in the garden nearest the house. She put on her raincoat and rubber boots and went for a closer look. From the perennial garden, still partially covered in snow, patches of yellow and purple beckoned. She squelched over the wet lawn to look. Crocuses! Then she walked around to the front of the house. More crocuses! She suddenly felt very Easter-like. She breathed in the damp fresh mild air.

She waited until nine, then made the phone calls she'd promised Andrew. Everybody was happy to come. Gerry counted on her fingers. Cece and Bea, Blaise, Prudence, her, Doug, David, Andrew and Markie. And the birthday girl, of course. Ten. She felt a sinking feeling in her stomach as she thought of Mary and Margaret. Andrew wouldn't invite his mother and sister to Cathy's birthday party, would he? She quickly phoned his number.

"Mm? Hello?" he groggily answered.

"Oh, Andrew, sorry if I woke you. I have the guest list for Monday." She quickly rattled off the names, adding, "So I make that ten. Is that right?"

Silence at the other end told her he was thinking. "Yee-es. There may be someone else coming, though." His voice lowered. He must have consulted Markie because there was a reciprocating mumble and laugh. Gerry ground her teeth together, wondering how she could get through an afternoon with Mary or Margaret, or both.

"When will you know, Andrew? Because maybe I should make a larger cake."

He laughed. "It's Prince Charles, Gerry. We thought it would make Cathy happy to bring him, but even Cathy wouldn't feed her dog cake."

Though Gerry could have contradicted him with the past evidence of her own eyes, she was so relieved she just laughed. "So ten people and one prince. Awesome. Go back to sleep." Duty done, she could now drive to her first author book signing.

The drizzle became a downpour and she slowed her car as the windshield wipers tried to keep up. Eventually, she pulled over under an overpass and sat there, hazard lights blinking, until the torrent diminished.

As a result, she was ten minutes late. When she rushed into the mall and found the CRAS volunteers just setting up, she was relieved. "Oh, look at the kittens," she cooed. A cage of half a dozen assorted kittens was prominently displayed on one table. On another, a few stacked cages held individual adult cats.

"I'm Jean Delamar," one stout elderly woman said, sticking out her hand. "We're grateful for your participation."

"Oh, it'll be fun!" enthused Gerry.

"Think so?" the woman replied, her face grim. She gave Gerry a few feet of one end of the adult cats' table for her books, and a chair. "I suggest you stand as much as possible. People take more notice. Let me introduce you to the cats."

Each cage came with a name tag telling the age and gender of its occupant. As Jean rattled them off, Gerry looked into the cats' empty eyes. Oh no, she thought, I'm going to want to adopt them all.

They moved to the cage of kittens. The contrast couldn't have been greater. The babies staggered around, pawing each other. One little fellow dozed in the cat litter box. Jean reached in, dusted him off and gently laid him onto a blanket. The kitten stood, stretched and fell over. "Don't worry about these guys," she said. "They'll probably all be gone by the end of the day. Talk up the adult cats, especially to any older people who seem interested. Want a coffee?"

When Gerry eagerly nodded, Jean strode off towards a nearby café. The other volunteers, a mother and daughter named Heather and Miriam, introduced themselves and seemed very nice, quiet people. They set out the CRAS pamphlets and waited.

Gerry remembered her books. She unpacked about ten copies and set them on the table. Jean returned with their hot drinks and each of the volunteers examined a copy of *The Cake-Jumping Cats of Dibble.*

Gerry sipped her coffee and waited nervously to hear what they thought. A muffled laugh escaped the daughter, Miriam. "Why it's *funny*," she said.

Her mother looked up and smiled. "Yes. I love the illustrations."

Jean sniffed. "Very good. I'll take a copy if you've any left at the end of the day."

"Oh good. I have more in the car. I just thought twenty would be a good number to start with." Jean grunted.

"Oh, Mommy! Look at the kitties!" Excited laughter dragged the CRAS volunteers away.

As the rainy morning wore on, the mall began to fill. It was the Easter weekend. There was a petting zoo at the other end of the mall and people brought their children to look at the bunnies and chicks, lambs and ponies before they did their shopping.

Gerry found herself discussing the merits of adult cats versus kittens with various people, and trying to sell her book as a fundraiser. It was harder than she thought.

Some people just wanted to handle the cats. They would hold one for a few minutes, then return it to her and walk away. Some just wanted to talk. Some were positively annoying.

One woman stood there for at least ten minutes, holding one of Gerry's books, blocking access for any others who might have wished to look at them, and telling Gerry all about a trip she'd taken years before to a Caribbean isle, and the many feral cats that had been living in miserable conditions there. Then she started listing all the reasons why she couldn't adopt a cat.

Jean got Gerry out of that situation. "Miss Coneybear," she called, "perhaps you'd like to take that break now." With relief, Gerry grinned and went to do her shopping elsewhere in the mall. It was noon and she'd sold two books. Oh well, she thought, at least the ten bucks I've made so far pays for my gas here and back.

Two more hours and three more book sales later and she was full of admiration for the volunteers. They'd found homes for four of the kittens and one adult cat. Heather and Miriam smiled and seemed genuinely interested in the people who stopped. Jean, while brusque with the humans, had real tenderness for the cats. At three o'clock, in a lull in the foot traffic past their tables, she took a black shorthair out of its cage and put it in Gerry's arms. "This is Seymour," she said. "He needs some attention."

Gerry sat down and started stroking the cat. He began a quiet purr and settled on her lap, facing away from her, but she could see by his ears that he was aware of her. She spoke softly. He sighed and lowered his head to her knees.

For some reason, she felt her throat tighten and her eyes fill with tears. Jean handed her a tissue. "Yeah, sometimes one of them gets me that way. And Seymour's a nice fellow. Seven years old. One owner who's just gone into a long-term care facility." She snorted. "No cats there, of course. God forbid the old people should have any companionship."

"Philosophers," Gerry said.

"Eh?" Jean looked startled.

"The thing about cats. That I admire. They're so rational. If they're hungry, they cry. If they're happy, they purr." She stroked the top of Seymour's head.

"He's only got one eye," Jean blurted.

"Really?" Gerry half-turned the cat. He blinked. "It's hard to see where — oh." The eye — what was left of it — was clouded.

"As far as I can tell from the owner, she tried to save money by treating it herself when he injured it. By the time she took him to the vet, it was too infected to save." Gerry silently stroked the cat. "I'd give you a special price," Jean began tentatively.

Gerry's mouth dropped open. "Don't you know I already have cats?"

"That's why I'm suggesting it," Jean said crisply. "We all have cats." Her eyes narrowed. "How many do you have, anyway?"

Gerry smiled and took a deep breath before she rattled off their names. "Bob, Lightning, Min Min, Harley, Kitty-Cat, Mouse, Blackie, Whitey, Jay — she's my kitten — Cocoon, Winston, Franklin, Joseph, Ronald, Mother, Max, Runt, Jinx and Monkey. I had twenty but one died and another one was adopted by my neighbour. Then I fostered five kittens — I only kept one of those — so we were twenty-three for a while. But nineteen now. I have nineteen cats." She thought she'd put up a strong defence.

It was Jean's turn to try to raise her slack jaw. Then she rallied. "Oh. So you won't notice one more." She looked admiringly at Gerry. "I thought I was something. I have three of my own monsters and foster others who are waiting to be adopted. If you don't take him, I'll be hosting Seymour until he is." She paused. "Half-price. Seventy-five bucks."

Gerry hesitated. Seventy-five bucks was the profits from selling fifteen books! Then she felt ashamed. Look what she'd been given: the house, money, a Paul-Émile Borduas painting that, even if it was stolen, would bring her insurance money.

Seymour decided her. He circled on her lap and wound up snuggling his nose into her hip. Gerry cupped his body with both hands.

Jean watched approvingly and nodded. "Now, because he's a new cat, your cats — some of them, anyway — may have to spar with him. You know, adjust the pecking order. Just let them get on with it and don't show him any special attention."

"How do you know I'm taking him?" Gerry's voice rose in incredulity, both at Jean's presumption and her own foolishness — for even considering it.

"Huh," was the response. "I know."

Heather and Miriam smiled sympathetically at Gerry. Miriam pulled a carrying case out from under a table while Heather handed Gerry a clipboard, form and pen. "I'd like to buy two copies of your book," she said kindly. "One for us and one for a friend who loves cats."

"Thank you," Gerry said faintly.

"You can return the cat carrier next time you come to sell your book. We'll be at the Central Mall next weekend. We have a circuit of malls we go to in winter. In the summer it's nicer because we can set up at farmers' markets and street fairs."

By four they were wearily packing up. The kittens were gone but four adult cats were left. Heather and Miriam took two and Jean took two to look after for the next week. Gerry, who had read the CRAS pamphlet during the day, and now knew that besides trying to find homes for the cats, the volunteers also responded to calls to trap and neuter stray cats, and took them to their veterinary appointments, said impulsively, "You people are saints!"

"Somebody's got to do it," Jean replied gruffly and waved goodbye.

Before she left the mall, Gerry took a few copies of her book to the bookstore there. The clerk couldn't promise to display them but let her leave them and gave her the name and number of the store's manager.

She was famished and bought a coffee and some chewy white chocolate macadamia nut cookies to eat in the car. With her new cat, she stepped out into a fine April drizzle.

Best to try to forget the previous night's hissings and meows, she thought, finally rising at six after listening to Seymour pacing and crying outside her bedroom for an hour.

The door was open but every time Seymour tried to enter, Bob leapt off the bed, tail fluffed and hackles upraised. "Right!" Gerry said, and retrieved Seymour. She climbed back into bed with him. "Bob, this is Seymour, your new best friend. Seymour, I don't care when you think breakfast should be; in this house we rarely rise before eight. Thank you!"

Speech delivered, she turned her back on both of them and prayed for a few more hours of sleep. It was not forthcoming. Seymour tried to circle and nestle on the bed. Alarming growls came from Bob's side of Gerry's prone figure. At her feet, Lightning was moving restlessly, while Jay, never the soundest sleeper, thought it might be fun to clamp onto the top of Gerry's head.

"I'm in cat hell!" roared Gerry, sitting up suddenly. Both Jay and Lightning scooted from the room. Bob and Seymour were unaffected, caught up in their male dominance displays.

"Oh, I give up," Gerry muttered, turned on a lamp and reached for her book. She'd found a row of novels by Mary Wesley and was enjoying reading about their characters' eccentric life choices in the early and mid-twentieth century.

After a chapter or two, she realized Bob and Seymour were both asleep, laid her book aside and joined them.

She wouldn't have been so tired if the night before she hadn't gotten interested in illustrating Aunt Maggie's stories and started going through old family photograph albums looking for street scenes and houses in old Lovering. She was thrilled to discover that the main road had been unpaved until the thirties, and that other roads she travelled on had been mere farm tracks.

So if she was sketching, say, scenes from "The Singing Milkman," she could make it much more bucolic than she'd previously imagined.

As usual, research proved time consuming, and it had been after midnight when she went to bed.

"So what do I have to do today, cats? Besides cater to your every whim?" She was drinking her coffee in the living room and trying to ignore Seymour, which was difficult, as he was crouched under her chair, and every so often made an effort to come out and jump onto her lap. At which point, one of the other cats — Bob, one of the boys, Min Min — would rush him, growling. Most of the other cats had ranged themselves around the room — audience or jury? She didn't know.

She picked up Jay and Ronald, the youngest of the cats, and gave them some love, hoping the other cats would see this and leave poor Seymour alone. Eventually, the feline need for post-breakfast sleep kicked in, and some cats left the arena for quieter places in the house, while those that remained with Gerry found their eyelids drooping irresistibly. When she peeked under her chair, even Seymour was dozing.

"So. What *do* I have to do?" She wished: nothing. As a self-employed artist, she rarely took a day off. "But I will today," she vowed, rising, and dumping Jay and Ronald on the hearth rug.

She would go to church. She hadn't been since Christmas. She hummed as she looked for something Easterish to wear. But warm. She settled on beige pants, a pretty yellow shirt with little wooden beads on the front and a pale green sweater. Putting on her lightest coat and tan loafers, she crossed the road and walked the short distance to St. Anne's church, listening to the bell calling the faithful.

For once she was on time. The organist doodled quietly on the keyboard. Easter lilies shone from each window aperture. She took a deep breath and relaxed. Then the organ broke into "Alleluia" and the service began.

Afterwards, she picked her way carefully between flat melting sheets of ice to the memorial wall at the back of the graveyard and lightly touched the names there. Her mother. Her father. She noticed a new plaque next to her mother's, that of a stranger. Should she reserve a spot on the wall for herself? She shook herself. She was being gloomy. She was only twenty-six! Who knew what life had in store for her? And she had to make a cake. She turned away from the wall and strolled home, envisioning preparing the cake batter, whipping cream and shaping marzipan ducks. Do all that and let the cake cool. Then it would just be assembly.

Seymour trailed after her into the kitchen. She quietly closed the door. "Okay, buddy, help me make a cake." He'd obviously done so before, dozing at the end of the counter as Gerry cracked eggs, beat butter and sugar and sifted flour. He had as rotten a night's sleep as I did, she realized. Probably worse.

He woke up when she used her electric beater to froth the egg whites. Cake in the oven, she whipped the cream and put it in the fridge. "Now for the fun part," she said, unwrapping the marzipan.

She began adding a very little bit of yellow food dye to the light beige almond paste. "Duck yellow," she proudly announced, when she'd achieved the right hue. The phone rang, making both her and Seymour jump. She quickly washed her hands. "Hello?"

"Gerry. It's Blaise. I just wanted to remind you to feed the cats this afternoon. Around four or five would be fine."

"Can do, Blaise. Good thing you phoned me. Have a nice Easter. See you tomorrow." She'd just dug her fingers into the delightfully malleable marzipan when the phone rang again. It was Doug.

"I'm taking the boys to be with their mother and grandmother this afternoon. You want to hang out? Here, for a change?"

If Gerry had been a cat, she'd have begun purring. "I've been missing you," she said softly. "What time?"

"About two? I have to pick them up after supper."

Gerry thought about a cat-free day. "I have to come home and feed the cats. And Blaise's two."

"Your life is ruled by cats," Doug teased.

"And I just adopted another one," Gerry said sadly.

"What!? Tell me about it when I see you. Okay?"

"Okay." Now that she had something to look forward to, she modelled her marzipan ducks with enthusiasm. A knock at the door surprised her.

It was Blaise's nephew with the key to his uncle's house. "Of course!" Gerry said, smacking her forehead. She extended her hand where the squashed decoration wobbled. "Duck?" The bemused man declined.

Baking finished, she reluctantly set up the mouse traps in the lower kitchen cupboards, talking to mice she imagined might be listening. "Okay, you guys, these are unforgiving contraptions, I've heard, so you might want to avoid this part of the house in future." Hah. Fat chance, she thought, what with all the baking and cat feeding in this room. The crumbs must be tremendous.

During a long soak in the bath, with the usual assortment of curious visitors coming and going, she tried to let her mind calm down. But it jumped restlessly like a flea.

Prudence's husband. Was he out? Gerry's lost painting. What would happen now? How long would it take for the insurance to pay out? What remained of the money Aunt Maggie had bequeathed to her was best left in her savings account for emergencies. Could she keep her chequing account topped up, thus ensuring The Maples and the cats stayed afloat?

Her brain darted down a pleasurable alleyway as she contemplated drawing the house sailing down the river with assorted cats hanging out of windows and clinging to the roof. Then reality reasserted itself. Would she have to dip into her emergency fund for veterinary expenses? What had she been thinking of, getting another cat? Her comic strip, her art class, her cake, her afternoon with Doug, all jumbled in her mind and she dozed off.

When she awoke she felt better. She dressed and surprised the cats by giving them half their supper as a late lunch. She washed the twenty little saucers and left them to dry. She went next door and did the same for Graymalkin and Ariel, petting them as they ate. "Sorry guys, more time later."

Now she wouldn't feel guilty when she missed everyone's usual supper times. With a light heart, she drove to Doug's.

10

"What are you bringing to tomorrow's feast?" Gerry asked. As she was sitting upright in bed, munching on apple and cheese, wearing one of Doug's flannel shirts, he didn't immediately answer.

"I said — "

"I know. I know. I was just admiring that shirt. I never realized how soft it is before." He reached over to stroke the fabric.

She grinned at him. "I may have to keep it."

"Sure. And I'm bringing what you're eating: cheeses and a few pears, apples, grapes."

"Nice. I made my cake and just need to assemble it. Tonight, I guess." She lay back in the bed and sighed. "This is nice. Doug?"

"Mm?"

"How do you do it? Keep it going? The boys, the house. Your art. All your odd jobs."

He lit a cigarette and inhaled deeply, exhaling away from Gerry. "The boys because I love them. The house because I'm handy. My art because it bugs me if I don't do it. And the jobs support the whole thing. It's not so bad. We don't pay rent."

"No, just heat, electricity, and maintenance," Gerry reminded him.

"Yes, but that's fair, don't you think? After all, it's Mary's house. She and Geoff were letting Margaret live here free. Now it's for the boys." He added regretfully, "If I could afford to give Mary something, I would."

"And your art? You were going to show me what you're working on."

He went to an art table under a gabled window, returning with a big piece of cardboard. Gerry examined the swoops and swirls drawn in black marker. "Doug, I can make neither head nor tail of this."

"I know. That's because this is one of the early designs, just for me. It's three-dimensional." He brought more renderings over to the bed. "This is one side. This is the reverse of that one. It's meant to be walked around. It'll be on a pedestal under which the electrics can disappear." He pulled up a final drawing. "And this is the design with colour added."

She gasped. The finished piece consisted of short lengths of red, orange and hot pink, all bent, shaped and assembled into a somewhat transparent sphere. "Like a hollow ball of wool!" she said excitely.

"Exactly. I've already made about three quarters of the pieces. I'm doing it the cheap way: painting the outside of the tubes instead of paying for coloured glass."

"How do you actually make it, Doug?"

"You heat a glass tube with a torch and bend it with tongs. It's like glass-blowing. You cork one end of the tube and blow into the other. Then you can weld different coloured tubes to each other. Finally, you inject the tube with inert gas. The colour depends on the type of gas and the colouring of the tube combining. You weld the cathodes on the ends of the finished product and ionize the gas by applying a high voltage through the cathodes."

"And the colours of this one? Are they neon?"

"Yup."

"Where is it? When can I see it?"

"Oh, it's in a neon sign maker's workshop in LaSalle. I'd rather wait until it's finished for you to see it."

"Are you going to sell it?"

"That would be great, but I've no clue how to market it. I'm hoping Malcolm — it's his workshop — will find me a client. Maybe a fancy restaurant. Or a nightclub."

"Amazing. You are so talented. What time is it, Doug?"

"Time for this, Gerry. And this."

They woke up to the sound of car doors slamming and then the front door of the house opening, and the murmur of the boys.

Doug cursed and dressed quickly. "They were supposed to phone me for a ride."

Gerry looked sadly at the remains of their lovely afternoon: the plate of food, the artwork, the rumpled bed. With a quick kiss, Doug left her and ran downstairs. Time for him to put on his parenting hat while she had the responsibility of two houses of cats to feed and a cake to decorate.

As Gerry pulled up her pants by the bedroom window, she saw Margaret reverse Mary's car, stare at her former home for a moment, then drive slowly down the long pothole-filled driveway. Poor Margaret. Based on what Gerry knew about Mary, she'd probably over-indulged in Easter wine and left Margaret holding the basket, as it were.

She made a quick hi and bye to the boys in the kitchen. David and Geoff looked unhappy and confused, while the eldest, James, seemed angry. "Call you later," Doug said. She wondered what could have thrown them all into such a state. She glumly answered her question: Mary and Margaret. She hoped her presence hadn't aggravated the situation.

When the Mini finally bumped onto the main road, there was Margaret in Mary's car, pulled over, waiting.

Gerry drove home at the speed limit, though she would have much rather exceeded it. Margaret followed her the whole way, even pausing at the end of Gerry's driveway after she'd turned in. When Gerry opened her car door, Margaret accelerated away.

A shaken and sweaty Gerry let herself into her house. She knew what Margaret was capable of. Suddenly, the fact that an unpunished murderer was on the loose, a fact she'd been trying to distract herself from with all her various activities, could no longer be ignored. She was terrified. And there was nothing, in the absence of any proof of Margaret's previous crime that she or anyone else could do.

So she did the only thing she could: she fed the cats.

Then she walked across her slushy backyard, trying to enjoy the little ephemeral spring blooms, to the gate in the hedge that separated her property from Blaise's, and let herself in, fed those cats and gave them some attention, then went home and opened a can of baked beans and made toast.

She assembled her pretty Easter cake, putting it on a pale green glass raised cake stand. The cake was iced light orange and she'd modelled a green marzipan nest sprinkled with green-dyed coconut to contain two of her bright yellow ducklings, while the remainder marched around the top of the cake. Their tiny orange feet and bills had been tricky. She cleaned up the kitchen and went to bed with a cup of tea and her novel. She'd let Mary Wesley's descriptions of the antics of the landed gentry of England between the two world wars take her mind off all her worries.

When she woke up Easter Monday, it was to a strange muffled silence. She looked out the window. A lot of snow had fallen during the night and thick fluffy flakes were still descending.

She spent a quiet morning working on greeting cards that featured her cartoon hero, Mug. Designs for Mother's Day and Father's Day cards had long been sent to the card company. Now she was working on graduation and general birthday cards.

She drew Mug, wearing a tiny mortarboard and gown and clutching a miniscule diploma, beaming as he stood on a human-sized mortarboard. All you saw of the human was its forehead and a giant hand preparing to lift and toss the hat. The text said "It wasn't easy!" You knew what was coming.

When you opened the card, there was Mug, sitting on his bum, dishevelled but still smiling and still holding his now crumpled diploma. Now the text read "But you did it!"

Not bad, she thought, leaning back. She squeaked when she saw the time. She changed, ran over to Blaise's, escorted him to Andrew's, ran home and got her cake. As she entered Andrew's house for the second time, she heard a car slowing on the road behind her. It accelerated before she could identify its driver. But how many people in Lovering drove a ten-year-old grey BMW like her Aunt Mary's?

"You look grim," a cheerful Andrew observed, carefully taking the cake so she could remove her coat. "This looks great!"

"You didn't invite your mother or sister, did you?" She spoke sharply.

Andrew looked startled. "I'd hardly do that," he replied. "Mother doesn't approve of my lifestyle choices. Why?"

"Because I think I just saw your mother's car drive slowly by."

"It is the main road, Gerry," he said gravely.

"Of course." She tried to push the incident from her mind. "The food smells wonderful."

Andrew's eyes twinkled. "Let's go annoy the chef."

Blaise was seated in the kitchen doing just that, telling Markie, who was too polite to turn away, all about his outing the previous day. "So nice to visit Montreal," he said, "but so exhausting."

"Blaise, let me get you a drink," interrupted Andrew. He mixed four mimosas and they toasted the day. Markie went back to work.

More guests arrived: Doug, with, surprisingly, Geoff Jr. as well as David. The boys carried plates of cheese and fruit. Bea and Cece had picked up Prudence. Between them they'd brought a large mixed salad and three bottles of wine. It promised to be a lively lunch.

Bea flung her arms around Gerry. "Hello, stranger! How are you?"

Gerry grinned. "Good. How was your concert?"

"Edifying. You should have come. There were hot hors d'oeuvres before and dessert after."

"Aha! Some music lover you are. You just went for the food!"

Cece leaned in to their conversation. "Don't tell anyone, eh?" Bea cuffed him on the shoulder.

Gerry wondered whether she should ask Prudence about her husband but she seemed all right, arranging snacks on the dining room table.

At ten to one Markie announced the food was basically ready. It just remained for someone to keep a lookout for Cathy by the front window. David volunteered and Geoff Jr. went with him. The adults spoke in hushed voices, waiting.

Doug came over to Gerry and squeezed her fingers. "How are you?" They moved into Andrew's formerly sparsely furnished living room, now equipped with floor-to-ceiling shelves featuring Aunt Maggie's ceramic collection, her bequest to him.

"Oh, you know, worried about you and the boys. Why were they so upset last night? Was it because I'd been there?"

"What? Oh, no. Gosh, no. They barely noticed you. No. It's Mary. She doesn't want to leave her big house, so she's decided to take it off the market, sell the one the boys and I are living in and use that money to live on."

"She's throwing her grandsons out of their home?" Gerry couldn't believe even Mary could be this selfish.

"Yeah, but no. She's invited them all to move in with her. And since Margaret is now living there, it makes a kind of weird sense. To reunite the boys with their mother." He looked miserable.

"But neither of them is fit. To look after anybody," Gerry hissed fiercely.

Doug looked taken aback. "I know. But actually, only David is underage. The other two can decide for themselves. And any judge would let David also decide for himself. That's why they were all confused when they got home yesterday." Now it was his turn to look angry. "Trust Mary to use Easter Sunday to stir up a nest of hornets."

Gerry became aware of Prudence flapping her arms silently in their direction and shushed Doug. David and Geoff Jr. rushed into the kitchen and Andrew went to let Cathy in. As he took her coat and Markie clanked a few plates and smiled at the quiet guests, Andrew said, "We thought we'd just eat in the kitchen."

As he led Cathy towards them, they heard her say, "I see a lot of cars parked at Gerry's. What do you think — ?" and everyone jumped and yelled "Surprise!"

Cathy jumped too and Prince Charles woofed in startled displeasure. "It's all *right*, Charles," his mistress assured him before welling up and clutching her throat with emotion. "Oh, you're all so sweet!"

She surveyed the food, hot out of the oven. "Oh, Markie, you shouldn't have! Oh, sweetie! Ham the way Mum used to make! And her scalloped potatoes!" She clasped her much taller sister, then went around kissing all the other guests.

"All right, everybody, out! Out!" cried Markie, flapping her apron at them. "You," she said to Prudence. "You look useful. You can stay." Prudence smiled smugly and put on an apron.

Everyone else trooped out into either the living room or the dining room where the table had been set up buffet style. They helped themselves to snacks and fresh drinks until Markie and Prudence started bringing in the main courses.

Besides the ham and potatoes, Markie had done asparagus in hollandaise sauce and green beans with almonds, *and* carrots with lemon butter, honey and thyme. It was a feast! Obviously, like her sister, Markie could cook. They loaded their plates and were soon all digging in.

Doug was having an earnest conversation with lawyer Cece so Gerry turned and found David and his brother Geoff at her elbow. "Good food, eh?" she commented. They nodded. Then, knowing that David at least was her friend, she asked, "How was it Sunday at your grandmother's?"

The boys exchanged a look. Then David burst out with, "It was so weird!" He stopped, looking guilty.

Knowing how torn between his parents he must feel, Gerry gently said, "I'm sorry."

He looked at his brother. Geoff just shrugged and kept eating. David continued, "Gramma Mary had hidden Easter eggs! Around the house! And outside. And she gave us baskets when we arrived and told us to go hunt for them." He paused.

Gerry, picturing Mary's probable state of inebriation and seventeen-year-old David, eighteen-year-old Geoff and twenty-year-old James's shock at this attempt at infantilizing them, couldn't suppress a giggle. "I'm not laughing at you," she hastily reassured the two young men. "I'm trying to imagine your faces. It's pretty bizarre."

Geoff looked pained. "I know, right?" It was the first time he'd voluntarily spoken to her. Gerry felt pleased and chose her response carefully. "And did you have a nice meal?"

"Not like this one!" Geoff replied. "Gramma bought a couple of rotisserie chickens with fries."

"And your mother? How is she doing?"

"I don't know," David said doubtfully. "She wants us to live with her at Gramma Mary's big house. At least, Gramma Mary said she does. Mum was pretty quiet." His brow wrinkled and he looked tense.

Gerry soothed him. "You must do what you think is best — for yourself, David."

"What choice do we have?" Geoff interjected. "She's got all the money. Dad can't afford — " He stopped, looking uncertain.

"I know about your dad's financial situation," Gerry was beginning, when cries from the living room told them Cathy was beginning to open her presents. "We should go," she indicated with a jerk of her head.

"Gereee! Your cute book! I shall read it to Charles tonight. And the lovely soap! Thank you!" They exchanged kisses and Gerry moved away from Cathy as the next gift was picked up and exclaimed over. Then Prudence appeared with the cake and they all sang at the top of their voices. There was champagne with the cake, or tea or coffee for the more temperate. Gerry, not having to drive, enjoyed the wine. It went well with her orange-flavoured confection. Much ado was made by the guests over her Easter ducklings before they were devoured.

By three-thirty, Blaise was tired so, after they made their good-byes, Gerry walked him across the street, made him comfortable in his kitchen recliner and left him dozing, a cat on each knee. She walked through Blaise's backyard and to her own house.

Sometime during the day the snow had stopped falling. Gerry looked at the lake, mostly clear of ice, grey-blue with tiny ripples shimmering on its surface. The crocuses were bravely holding their own, though snow dusted. They'd tightly closed themselves in defence. She turned to face the back of her house. Broken egg was smeared on all the lower windows and some of the upper ones. And BITCH had been spray-painted in giant red letters on the siding.

Gerry's mind flew to the moment when, almost a year ago, she'd discovered someone had keyed her car. And now, as it had then, her stomach clenched.

She went up to one window. The egg was still moist. Someone had done this just moments before, while she'd been at Cathy's party. She was glad Geoff Jr. had accompanied David and Doug to lunch. That meant she only had to suspect one of Doug's sons: James. Or his mother.

Grimly, she went inside to get a pail of water.

PART 3

TORMENT

Kitten woke as cold air enveloped the bed. Top Cat and Scaredy-Cat were awake too but didn't seem bothered. The girl snored gently.

For a moment, the calico wraith coldly eyed Kitten, who was tucked in her favourite place above the girl's head on her pillow, then jumped from atop the girl's stomach. The girl muttered and turned onto her side. Kitten followed the calico out of the room.

The two young ghosts from before — the dark man and the pretty woman — were examining portraits hanging in the hall and didn't take any notice of either cat.

The calico streamed down the stairs, leaving cooler air where she'd passed. Kitten sidestepped the wraith's path and kept to one side of the staircase.

They entered the dining room. Most of the other cats began to stir. The ghastly-faced man and his relatives sat around the table holding each other's wispy hands. That the table was huge, thus ensuring they had to elongate the filmy stuff of which they were made, only added to the eeriness of the scene.

As the two cats moved through the passageway that connected the dining and living rooms, Kitten felt the temperature decrease and the hairs along her spine prickle.

Once in the living room, the calico leapt onto the lap of the tall woman who was seated in one of the rocking chairs near the hearth. Her mother sat in the other chair and the two held hands. They, like the other ghosts, seemed to be waiting.

Kitten began to vibrate.

It was one thing to crouch in a dark corner listening for the delicate scrabble of mouse-feet and then to inch ever closer to the source of the scrabble before the final pounce.

It was quite another to sense the spectral tension in the house and to hunker down under the living room table, wondering what it was all about. As the tension built, Kitten's nerve snapped. She yowled.

At that moment something like a branch in a storm slapped wetly at the back window above the table where Kitten was sheltered. She jumped from the floor to a chair and then onto the table.

A male form was plastered against the glass. Tall, red-haired, he dripped with water. Water trickled from inside his distorted angry mouth.

Kitten ricocheted off the table back onto the chair and dived under the table again. She closed her eyes but was aware of cold air coming from where the two women and cat sat. They would protect her. They would keep the wet thing outside.

She opened her eyes and saw smoke outside the front window of the room. It looked like the house was on fire! She dashed from under the table onto the bench, put her front paws on the windowsill and looked out.

An old, old man was pressed to the glass, as if seeking a crack through which his vapour could enter. Kitten smelled sulphur. She recognized him from the painting in the foyer. The painting two of the other inside ghosts had treated disrespectfully. The old man raised a spectral rock.

Kitten climbed a curtain and batted frantically at the glass as the rock made contact. The window broke into a dozen wispy fragments and she felt the girl's hands on her body, detaching her claws from the curtain material then holding her close.

As the girl turned from the window, Kitten heard a motor start and a car drive away.

The calico wraith heard it too and went berserk, writhing and spitting as her owner tried to soothe her. She broke free, detaching her wisps from those of the woman, and streamed toward the window where Kitten and the girl were.

Kitten hid her eyes in the crook of the girl's arm as the calico's cold essence enveloped them. Then there was the soothing smell and taste of warm milk and the ghosts disappeared.

11

Gerry hadn't much enjoyed this train ride from Lovering to Montreal. Though, when she arrived, she stuck to her rituals, this time buying a full breakfast of bacon and eggs and taking it out onto the concourse, there to sit and eat. She wondered what she might expect from the coming interview. Then she brightened. At least she had one positive thing to look forward to. She finished her snack and set off.

Bertie Smith's antique shop was at the edge of a tony neighbourhood on a side street, below a small art gallery. She walked down a few stairs and pushed open the door. Bells tinkled both at the front and rear of the shop.

Bertie himself pushed through a curtained doorway, wiping his mouth with a paper napkin. Gerry saw the familiar company logo on the napkin before he crumpled and pocketed it. "Another fast food fan, I see," she said and grinned.

His eyes twinkled and he sniffed. "Yes, well, it can't all be *haut monde*, can it? How are you, Miss Coneybear? And what brings you to my shop?" He took a pipe out of his vest pocket and began to fill it with tobacco.

"To be honest, Mr. Smith, I have some time to kill before I meet with Mr. Frey and I found your card, so… And I'm well, thank you. You?"

"I'm very well. So, as this is a social call, will you take a cup of tea?"

"Thank you. I think I will." He walked to the front of the shop, locked the door and flipped the sign to read *closed*, lit his pipe, then disappeared behind the back curtain. Gerry loitered in the shop. She picked up a ceramic frog. Cute. She looked at a ceramic mug or jug with a Beefeater's face. Horrible. Out the window she saw the feet of passersby. Here, in the city, most of the snow had melted and people were back to wearing shoes.

"Here we are." He beamed at her as he deposited a tray with tea things and a plate of cookies. He sniffed again as she took one. "You may call me Bertie."

"Gerry," she said.

"Bertie and Gerry," he joked. "Sounds like a comedy team. You don't mind the — ?" He held the pipe in the air between them.

"No. Go ahead. I like the smell." She added quietly. "But isn't it illegal?"

"My shop, my rules," he said. "When we're closed I do what I like."

The cookies were plain but very buttery. Gerry took a second. The tea was strong and good. "Do you have any advice or opinion as to what I should expect at Frey's?"

Bertie sniffed and blew his nose. He smiled. "Allergic. To dust. Figures, eh? Me working in antiques." Gerry smiled back. He continued, "I think if the news was good, they would have phoned you."

Gerry, who'd been leaning forward on the edge of her seat, wilted and sat back. "Yes, I thought the same, but it was Easter…and…"

Bertie rested his pipe in an ashtray, put his fingertips together and rested his chin on them. "You are entitled," he said slowly, "to a very detailed explanation from Frey. I suggest you take notes. That'll rattle them. Do you have writing materials?"

Gerry patted her knapsack. "I'm an artist. Always have paper and pens and pencils. So I take notes. But what do I want at the end of it?"

"Dates. Specifically, the date Frey's has or will submit an insurance claim, and all that contact information so you can follow up with the insurance company yourself. Not that you'll get much from them. Frey is their client. But it's good you seem involved."

Gerry had been making notes as he spoke. "This is very helpful. Thank you."

He cleared his throat. "Would you, that is, er, would you like to have lunch with me after your appointment? I'd like to hear about the meeting."

Gerry considered. "Well, the earliest train back to Lovering is at 2:30 and I will be hungry before that. All right. But we pay for ourselves, okay?"

"Agreed. Would you have any objection if I phoned Mrs. Stewart? She expressed an interest in your situation. Perhaps she'd be free to join us."

Gerry smiled. "Fine. I'd like to see her again. I'll come back here, then, shall I?"

He nodded. As she put on her coat, she looked up. There, high on a shelf, were assorted British Royal Family memorabilia. "Mugs," she said.

He looked up. "Oh yes? Any particular mug?"

"I have a friend who collects them. And I don't know which ones she already has."

He dragged over a stool and climbed up. He started passing down the mugs. She put them on a counter. He hopped down and sniffed. "Hm. These are pretty standard: all twentieth century: coronations, royal tours, anniversaries. Here's one she may not have." He handed Gerry an Edward VIII mug.

"I didn't even know there was an Edward VIII."

Bertie sniffed. "One of my namesakes. My mother gave me Edward for this king, the one who abdicated. To marry the divorced woman." He sniffed repeatedly. "When he left, she started calling me by my second name, Albert, after the second son who became George VI. He was known as Bertie among his family."

"It's awfully confusing — the names, I mean."

"Yes. Each prince has about four I think. Edward VIII was known as David to his intimates. To his wife. Wallis Simpson. People hated her." He put on a hearty British accent. "Very bad show, eh? What?" He switched back to his normal voice. "It's fifteen bucks. You can return it if she has one. Or exchange it for another."

Gerry nodded. "I'll take it. I'll get it later, okay?"

She walked briskly to Frey's, feeling much more confident. As before, she was scrutinized, showed her driver's licence and was tagged. Also her knapsack was searched. Mr. Frey himself came to greet her and this time the elevator went up.

It opened directly into his office. At one end of the room was a large window. "Go look," he urged. She crossed the room.

She had a view of the auction hall, now empty. "That's neat."

He seemed pleased. "It is, isn't it?" He motioned her to sit.

Gerry took a good look at him. William Frey was about fifty years old. He was short and chubby and his well-groomed hair was black with grey streaks. He wore a navy blue suit with a white shirt and green tie, and smelled of a pleasant cologne. She liked him. "So?" she asked.

He pulled a file closer. "So. We have traced the painting's movement from the time you brought it here to when it was discovered missing at the auction. Here is its history." He handed her a sheet of paper.

Gerry read the entries. It all seemed correct. She had a question, though. "When paintings enter or leave Frey's, they are checked, right? To make sure they really are that painting?" He nodded. "And who does that checking?"

"Well, one of our experts, of course."

"So one of your experts is the thief, no?" Gerry felt very daring to be making such an accusation to this nice dapper man.

He seemed unfazed. "One of our experts may have made a mistake." He pointed to two lines on the list. "The Borduas left us to be cleaned. Those are the dates when it left and when it returned. We suspect that's when someone may have slipped up."

"Perhaps." Then she remembered Bertie and Mrs. Stewart's reaction the day of the auction. "But, Mr. Frey, the Borduas is small. It could fit in this." She indicated her knapsack. "So someone at Frey's could have smuggled it out. Just saying."

His dismay showed on his face. "But I assure you, Miss Coneybear — "

She decided to take control of the interview. "Mr. Frey, what is the situation between Frey's and the insurance company?" She sat with pen poised over notebook.

"Ms. Adams has been dealing directly with them." He picked up his phone and asked Ms. Adams to join them. "Can I offer you any refreshment while we're waiting?" Gerry shook her head.

Ms. Adams swept in, giving Gerry a curt nod. Frey busied himself with some papers on his desk. "Can you fill us in on the insurance for the Borduas?" he asked.

Ms. Adams referred to her own file. "As per your instructions, Mr. Frey, we have delayed filing a claim until we carried out a thorough search."

"And?" he said.

"And, having done so and finding no trace of the painting, I suggest we claim."

"And inform the police, surely?" Gerry interjected.

Frey nodded, looking weary. "Yes. I suppose we must. Will you handle that,Ms. Adams?"

She bowed her head and left. Frey sighed. "It's not good for my house when things like this happen. People take their business elsewhere."

Gerry stood up. "I'm glad the claim will be filed. Have Ms. Adams send me a copy of the claim with contact information, please."

Frey stood, looking startled. "Of course, of course. I'm sorry, Miss Coneybear. We'll make it right."

Ironic, she thought, as her knapsack was searched in the foyer. The horse has already left the barn.

She marched back to Smith's Antiques, full of her thoughts and information. Bertie had his coat on. "Change of plan. Marion's invited us to lunch at her place." When Gerry expressed pleasure, he said, "Don't get your hopes up. It'll be soup from a packet and tinned meat sandwiches. Oh, well, I suppose she doesn't feel like going out." He handed her the mug, well wrapped in newspaper in a little bag.

"How do I know this is the same mug I examined earlier?" she teased with a smile.

Grimly, he replied, "You're learning."

As they walked, Bertie pointed out various small art galleries and antique shops, critiquing or validating their operators. "Too pretentious with inflated prices," was the verdict on one. "Not bad prices, but really, you could find his inventory at a good yard sale," was his judgement of another.

For Gerry, after a long cold winter spent in Lovering, it was all eye candy: the shops, the people in the streets. And the sounds of the city were stimulating as well: the distinctive noise of the buses; trucks' beepers going off as they backed into alleys; the croodling of pigeons nesting on building ledges.

Marion Stewart's apartment was on the top floor of an old building just up the hill from Bertie's shop and Frey's. She buzzed them in to a marble-floored foyer with mirrored walls and tropical plants in planters. A fountain gurgled near an arrangement of two chairs and a brass-edged glass coffee table.

Gerry raised her eyebrows. Bertie nodded. "Very expensive."

"Where do you live, Bertie?"

"Above the shop, on the third floor. I commute down the back stairs every morning."

They reached the fifth floor and stepped onto carpet that muffled their footsteps. From all the way down at one end of the corridor, their hostess beckoned.

"Marion."

"Bertie." The two exchanged air kisses.

"Mrs. Stewart." This kiss, from Marion to Gerry, was genuine.

"Call me Marion. And come in."

The apartment wasn't what Gerry had been expecting. For one thing it was so small. Or maybe it wasn't but was just overstuffed with furniture and ornaments. It was also dark, not because of a lack of windows, but because each had its shade half-pulled down, and a set of heavy curtains. The effect was fusty.

"I won't be a minute," Marion said, going off to the kitchen. Bertie and Gerry sat on a pale green sofa with elegant curved legs. The coffee and end tables were metal and glass. A small chandelier tinkled overhead. None of it was really to Gerry's taste but she could see it represented mid-twentieth-century décor of a certain high standard. Bertie sniffed.

"Pour us three sherries, would you, Bertie?" Marion called from the kitchen. Bertie brought the drinks from another room. Marion joined them and they sipped.

Surprisingly, Gerry found she liked the dry, woody flavour. "What is this?"

"Tio Pepé," the other two replied, simultaneously. They laughed. Marion continued. "Bertie, here, can recognize all manner of fine things. He's been well educated."

"By myself," he murmured politely, and inclined his head.

"It doesn't matter how one was educated as long as one was." She turned to Gerry. "And what was Frey's story?"

Gerry related her interview.

"Huh." Marion said. "No story at all. They don't know. Or they're afraid to dig too deep." She narrowed her eyes. "Like last time, eh, Bertie?"

"I wonder." He finished his sherry. "I shouldn't be too long away from the shop, Marion. Some of us have to work for a living." He winked at Gerry but she was too distracted by Marion's previous remark to react.

"What's this about the last time?"

"Let's eat and we'll tell you all about it," Marion said.

They processed into the small dining room. Another chandelier. A rectangular table surrounded by deep sideboards and an armoire. On the table were a soup tureen and a cloth-covered plate.

Gerry unfolded her napkin and gravely ate her soup, a cream of leek from a well-known instant brand. The sandwiches had been trimmed free of their crusts, the bread buttered and a thin smear of some reddish paste added. Actually, it wasn't a bad little meal, washed down with another glass of the dry sherry.

At the table, Marion kept the conversation light, reminiscing about her schooldays and life as wife to a Montreal businessman. No children were mentioned and Gerry assumed there weren't any.

After they'd eaten, their hostess shooed them back to the living room. Bertie sighed as he looked at his watch. "I should know by now. Marion won't be hurried." He rummaged for his pipe and tobacco. She entered pushing a trolley of coffee and *petits fours*.

"Now," Marion said after she'd served them. "How many have there been, Bertie?"

Bertie took out a little notebook. "Six," he said, "including Gerry's. One a year for the last six years."

Gerry's hand stopped halfway to her mouth. She put the square of pale blue iced cake back on her plate. "What!?".

She rode the train home in a daze. Marion and Bertie had been watching Frey's for years. Marion had used to sell some of her things at Frey's, but no more. Now she did so privately through Bertie. They'd noticed the pieces missing from sales when they were listed in the catalogue. It was always the same. A small painting worth a modest amount (by art world standards). No Van Goghs or Picassos that people would remark on. Always works by more obscure but still excellent painters, ones whose value could be expected to grow. When Bertie had asked around, he'd learned that the five previous missing paintings hadn't been withdrawn from the sales by their owners. And word was, the insurers, a different one each time, had always paid up. Presumably then the thief arranged to sell the painting to a collector who didn't mind keeping their acquisition secret. Marion and Bertie suspected someone at Frey's was setting up a wonderful retirement package for themselves. But who?

She wearily sat in the Mini parked at Lovering's station. She let the other commuters start their engines and leave. She remembered there should be a box of books waiting on the porch of her house and shifted into reverse. She would spend the evening planning how to sell the next hundred copies of *The Cake-Jumping Cats of Dibble*. She might need the money.

12

"Well! This is like the old days!" Gerry exclaimed brightly, thumping the ball of dough enthusiastically.

"Mm," Prudence agreed. She mixed brown sugar, cinnamon, melted butter and pecans, and spooned some of the mixture into the large rectangular pan. "I'm only helping because it's your teaching day. Otherwise — "

"Otherwise, I'm on my own. I know. But baking is so much easier if someone just shows you. Rather than trying to figure it out from a book." Enriched with warm milk and melted butter, the dough was stickier than usual. She made as if to plop it into the pan.

"Aaa! Stop!" Prudence put out a hand. "Point taken. Roll the dough out into a rectangle about half an inch thick. Smear on the rest of the filling. Roll up the dough into a tube and seal the ends and the long seam, like this. Now slice into fifteen equal pieces. We want three rows of five each."

Gerry stood over the dough, looking down. "Er, fractions were never one of my strengths."

Prudence handed her a sharp knife. "Do your best. When you put them in the pan they shouldn't touch. They have to proof once more. I'm going to vacuum. Meet me back here in an hour."

Gerry puzzled over the dough for a minute before she figured out how to divide it into three sections, then subdivide each of those into five. She laid the buns in the pan and covered it before cleaning the kitchen.

The sound of the vacuum faded as Prudence moved from the living room into the dining room. Gerry sat at her work table and made a few *Dibble*-related calls. Then she sorted the fresh copies of her book with their slick colourful covers into little piles, which she labelled and put into plastic bags. Tomorrow or the next day, she hoped to drive around, pick up money and drop off more books. She thought about doing another CRAS event. There wasn't much personal gain for her if she only sold a few copies. Considering that it took a whole day. She reminded herself it was for charity.

Her new cat Seymour walked into the room, hesitated, then headed for her. She looked around for other cats. Strangely, she and Seymour were alone. Guiltily, she picked him up and gave him a cuddle. "How's it going, sweetie? Are you settling in?" The kneading of her lap and the accompanying quiet purr gave her her answer.

She felt her tension drain away. She hadn't even known she was tense until the cat had comforted her. "Who's a good boy? Who's a lovely cat?"

Bob walked into the room. Gerry froze. Seymour's purr caught in his throat. Bob stopped on the hearth rug and groomed before jumping onto the table. Gerry put out a hand, palm up. "Bobeee," she coaxed. He sniffed her hand. Seymour turned on her lap so his back was towards Bob.

Apparently, Bob could live with that. He circled and settled on the list of prospective new locations for selling *Dibble* and blinked. Gerry leaned over and fondled his ears. "Thank you," she breathed. "Good cat." She made kissy sounds with her lips as Prudence passed behind her.

"Don't get up. I can see you're busy lion-taming." Prudence brought her the pan of pecan buns from the kitchen. "See how they've grown so they're just slightly touching?"

"Prudence! They look so professional!"

"I'll preheat the oven. Put them in for twenty-five minutes. Then tap for doneness. You want that hollow feel." She turned the oven on then reappeared with her lunch. As she plopped herself down at the table, she sighed.

"What?" Gerry asked, still trying to give two cats equal attention at the same time.

"I can't help — I can't help thinking." Prudence slowly unwrapped her sandwich.

"That's not a problem, surely. You *are* a wise woman."

"About Alexander." She stared down at her lunch.

Gerry had not been expecting this. Somehow she had presumed Prudence would do what she usually did — retreat into her shell and let it all be about Gerry. Already Gerry had monopolized the morning drive with the news of her house getting egged and tagged, and speculation about who could have done it; and, over their first cup of coffee that morning, relayed the suspicions of Marion and Bertie about Frey's. She felt ashamed and couldn't think what to say.

"What it's like living at the Mountainview. How he gets money. What he's eating. What he'll do now." Prudence turned her gaze on Gerry. "That cat's settling in." Seymour turned his blind eye to Prudence. "What happened to the eye?"

"An untreated infection. But it doesn't seem to bother him. It must be difficult for you, wondering."

"Wondering why I let him ruin my life, you mean," Prudence said bitterly.

"Prudence, when it comes to love, I'm as baffled as the next person." She added softly, "I assume you were in love?"

Prudence nodded. "Totally and completely. Swept away. He was the older brother of one of my friends. Three years older than me. 1965. I was seventeen. We got married in an apple orchard. You know, the old one on the trail up to the tracks. On the right of the path." Dreamily, she said, "It's all overgrown now." She bit into her sandwich. The oven pinged its readiness.

Gerry rose, dumping Seymour. He retreated to the hearth rug. "Sorry, bub. I'll put the buns in. I want my lunch too. Go on, Prudence."

Being unseen seemed to help Prudence confide. She raised her voice slightly. "I should have known. He was my first boyfriend. Handsome, strong jaw. Big brown eyes. He felt so strong — his body, I mean — when we hugged. And he had long red hair."

Gerry reappeared, having thrown together a peanut butter sandwich with a glass of milk. "You'd think the Vikings cruised up the Ottawa River, there are so many redheads in Lovering." She yanked one of her own locks by way of example.

"It's the ancestors. Coming from coastal England," Prudence explained. "And didn't your mother have red hair?" Gerry nodded. "I thought we were perfect for each other. What a mismatch. Mother tried to dissuade me, but when I got angry she just shut up and helped with the wedding.

"He smoked and drank. I did neither. I had a job — cashier. He was wasting time taking a few courses here, a few there. I tried to join him — you know, smoke a little pot, drink a little beer — but it wasn't me. I don't need to take the edge off. I like being clear-headed. I like to get up early. I like to work. I like a tidy house."

"I'm sorry, Prudence," Gerry said in a small voice.

"That was the worst of it. He said he was sorry. He'd fall asleep with a joint or cigarette burning in his hand, too drunk to notice. He'd have friends over during the day when I was at work and they'd make a mess. Then he'd say 'sorry' and expect it would all be good again. Except it had never really been good. I'd been in a dream."

Gerry drank some milk. Seymour jumped into Prudence's lap, startling her. Bob gazed at Gerry and slowly closed his eyes, before reopening them and then stepping carefully onto her lap. She asked, "How did it end?"

"When I realized his 'friends' were criminals. All of a sudden he'd have money — for beer, for drugs — and then he wouldn't. He'd be asking me for some. But I had to pay rent, buy groceries."

"Where were you living?"

"You wouldn't know it, but there are quite a few little apartments scattered around Lovering. We were above the paint shop. A kitchen–living room and one bedroom. Near the grocery store where I worked so we didn't need a car."

The oven timer pinged and both women removed their respective cats and rose to check the buns. A heavenly aroma and a uniform brownness (as well as the tap test) assured them of their being done.

"Out of the pan immediately or the topping will stay in the pan and not on the buns."

Gerry grasped the pan and flipped the buns out onto a rack. She gasped. A sticky brown glaze coated them. "Fantastic! The students will love these!" Impulsively, and not entirely because of the pecan buns, Gerry hugged Prudence.

Prudence clung. For a second. Then she commented briskly, "Hadn't you better get changed? They'll be here in twenty minutes."

Gerry mock-screamed and ran off to prepare. When she came back into the living room, Prudence had cleared the table and set up chairs. Gerry was gloating over the sticky buns when the doorbell rang.

That day she had the students copy from illustrations in books. She gave them the choice of what. Christine chose to imitate sketches of plants, of course, given her love of gardens. Sharon chose an architectural drawing of a church in Montreal, which she executed slowly and carefully, while Ben copied the cross-section of a car in a flyer Gerry had received from her dealer. Judy, rather naughtily, drew some of Gerry's cake-jumping cats, while June — well, June drew the same scene as the week before; people, mostly women, in 1920s garb, stood on Gerry's lawn facing the house, the lake behind them.

But this time, June had come a little closer and details of faces began to be visible. Also, it appeared that there were children in the scene, standing in the front row. As Gerry bent over, perplexed, June whispered, "Sorry. It's not copying. But it feels like copying." At that moment, Prudence entered with the tea and treats and the group, distracted, put down their pencils.

"Oo! You're spoiling us, Gerry," said Judith, taking a sticky bun.

Gerry smiled absently, thought fast and took June aside. "June, would it be possible for you to leave your drawing with me? Just for a week, say. And the one from last week, if you have it? I think you might be drawing from a photograph you may have seen in the past and I'd like to compare the drawings with my family's photo collection. Would that be okay?"

June nodded. "I don't need them," she said.

After tea and further discussion and critiques, the students left. As June made for her waiting car and her husband, Gerry pressed the bag containing the Edward VIII mug into her hand. "I saw this in Montreal and thought of you. I know you collect Royal Family memorabilia. I hope you like it."

A dazed June looked at the package, mumbled, "Thanks" and got into the car.

Gerry raced to where she'd put June's drawings but Prudence had beaten her. She stood, her mouth open, pointing at one figure. All she said was, "Mother."

Gerry and Prudence sat at the table, each clasping a mug of coffee. Before them was strewn every photo album The Maples possessed. None of them contained a photo that resembled June's drawings. Gerry reiterated her favourite explanation. "She must have seen it in the paper. From an archive, perhaps?"

Prudence shrugged. "I've never seen it before."

"It's odd that there's more detail in the second sketch." Gerry pointed. "In the first one we don't even see the children."

Again Prudence shrugged. "June Conway has always been different."

"You mean clairvoyant?"

"I mean paranoid. She rarely goes outside of her house, which I'm told is stuffed with objects she collects. The fact that she comes to your art class is a victory of sorts."

"Well, if she's sensitive to — ah — ghosts, but not possessed of a sturdy character like yourself — " Here Prudence snorted. Gerry continued, "She might find it overwhelming. I know I would." She looked around her. "There might be ghosts in this room right now. If there are, I don't want to be aware of them. It would be unsettling." She addressed the air in a louder voice. "No offence."

Prudence was pointing at the most recent drawing. "I recognize most of these children. They're all gone now, of course. Those are all the Catfords: Ellie, your grandmother; Edward, my father; Sylvia who married James Parsley and had six kids; Mary who married a Shapland — she'd be Doug's grandmother; and Andrew, who died in the Second World War. That's their mother Louise behind them. She died before I was born but my father had photos of her."

"Where's your mother, Prudence?"

Prudence tapped the image of a little girl who stood at the centre of the front row. "That's her."

"Wasn't she a twin?"

"Yes. But not identical. That's Isabelle, standing next to her. She died of influenza as an adult. Mother was never the same after that."

"She's not as defined in the drawing as your mother is. What I don't understand, Prudence, is, if these are our dead relations, where are Uncle Geoff and Aunt Maggie? Where are my parents?" Gerry shivered and pushed the sketch away.

Prudence shrugged. "Too recently dead? Not yet dead when this 'event' happened?"

Gerry heard a creaking noise behind her. She turned to see one of the rocking chairs moving back and forth, back and forth. The kitten Jay sat on the hearth and watched, her head moving in time to the chair's motion. She must have just jumped off it, Gerry thought.

The phone rang and she got up to answer it. "It's for you. Rita." Rita was one of Prudence's neighbours.

Prudence frowned. "Rita?" She listened. "I see. No. I'm coming now. Ask them to wait." She slowly returned the phone to the wall. "Can you drive me home? The police are at my house. They won't tell Rita why."

Gerry quickly fed the cats and they drove to Prudence's cottage. The police car was parked on the road so Gerry pulled into the driveway. "Should I — ?"

"You better come in," Prudence said calmly. "It can't be good news."

As the women exited the car, the police slowly got out of theirs. After introductions, all four trooped inside. Gerry and Prudence took off their coats and put them in the hall cupboard as the police stood quietly at the door.

Prudence sat in a wing chair by the front window. "Is it Alex?" she asked in a small voice, looking out the window. The police nodded.

"I'll make tea," Gerry said. Prudence indicated with her head that the kitchen was behind the living room.

She'd never yet been inside Prudence's house. The small entranceway opened onto the living room on the left and what she assumed were two bedrooms behind closed doors on the right. The kitchen was small, painted pale green with cream cabinets and trim; its little table looked out on a square backyard enclosed by a cedar hedge. A bird feeder on a pole completed the scene.

Gerry put on the kettle and rummaged for tea and mugs. She found a tray. When the kettle whistled she filled the humble brown teapot. She took a deep breath and went through.

13

"I can't believe what a change since Easter!" Gerry dragged the last bit of junk out of the shed and onto the parking pad. She'd parked the Mini in the semi-circular driveway at the front of The Maples behind Doug's car.

"I can't believe what a change since your birthday," he replied, hugging her. "Happy?"

She smiled and hugged back. "Very. Except for Prudence's ex-husband being found in a ditch. And someone egging my house. And my Borduas floating around somewhere in limbo. But with you, I'm happy. And on such a lovely day."

And it was lovely. The sun shone and a fresh breeze blew off the Lake of Two Mountains where ice floes floated on their way down the Ottawa River. The back lawn was three-quarters visible and little flowers were rising to transform it from tired brown and yellow grass to a blue carpet. Cardinals fluttered and called from the thicket next door as squirrels bounded from tree to lawn to tree.

"That reminds me." He bent over the open trunk of his car. "This is for you." Gerry looked blank as he lifted out a box on wheels, with an engine, a hose, a nozzle attachment and an extension cord. "I only rented it for half a day so get cracking."

"Huh?" she finally said.

"It's a power washer. It'll strip the graffiti off the back of the house. Along with the paint, unfortunately. When I return it, I'll pick up some paint for the wall. No, wait." He walked back to the pile of stuff they'd removed from the shed. "There's some leftover right here." He pried open the can. "Yup. Yellow. We're good."

Gerry stared at the machine. "Well, I have to plug it in." She did. "And attach its hose to the outside tap, I guess." She ran inside to open the water for the first time that spring. "Remind me to close that when we're finished." She dragged the machine around the back where the two-foot-high letters announced what sort of person someone thought she was. She aimed the nozzle at the wall, and shouting, "Die, graffiti!" slowly erased the letters.

Doug grinned. "I'll return it now, if you're quite done."

Gerry dropped the machine on the lawn. "I'll just get you some money for the rental."

"No, no, it's all right," he assured her.

"Doug! My house! My mess we're cleaning up!"

He hung his head. "I just feel uncomfortable taking your money."

"For a machine rental or working here today?"

"Both."

"Can't you think of it as Aunt Maggie's money, Doug? She did leave a sum specifically for the upkeep of the house. And you're the keeper-upper, or whatever it's called." She smiled wickedly. "She bequeathed you to me. Like the cats."

He pulled her close. "Am I nothing more than another cat to you, Madam?" It took a few minutes, but he eventually drove away, leaving Gerry looking at her shed.

Emptying it was necessary, as Doug and two local contractors, the Hudsons, were due to fix the roof at the back end where a tree had come down during a storm on Christmas Eve, driving some of Gerry's woodpile through the floor, which would also need repairs. She and Doug had stacked the remaining firewood on her parking pad. There wasn't very much left. Now she had to clean and store as much of the shed's junk as possible in her house. She started carrying stuff around to the front door. The foyer was as large as a room. The odd bits of furniture and tools would be fine in there. Once she had about half the shed's contents in front of the house on the circular drive by the front door, she moved her car back to the parking pad at the side of the house. Her stomach reminded her it was past lunchtime. She went inside.

She had just finished the construction of two towering smoked meat and mustard on rye sandwiches and was reaching for the dill pickles when a horrendous crash at the front of the house made her drop the jar.

It smashed on the floor at her feet. Luckily they weren't bare. And luckily no cats were there to be drenched with pickle juice or caught by bits of flying glass. As it was, her shoes and socks were soaked and the kitchen splattered.

She heard an engine and crunching noises. What the — ? The Hudsons (who had a history of breaking things) weren't due until tomorrow. She ran through the house toward the noise. She looked through the front door window.

A car, Aunt Mary's car, was backing up out of the circular driveway, a red-faced, grinning Margaret at the wheel, bits of crushed and splintered furniture and tools under the car and in the road.

Gerry shrieked, "Margaret! What are you doing!?" and raced out the front door onto the porch.

But Margaret wasn't finished. Having destroyed some of Gerry's possessions, she began on the house itself. She drove straight at one of the pillars that supported the porte-cochère, a relic from when the gentleman would pull up to the front door so the lady could alight, protected from all weather.

The wood cracked and buckled but held. Gerry shrieked again and retreated back into the house. Margaret backed up the by-now-battered car to take another run at the house.

Across the street, Andrew ran out of his house while Markie stood, open-mouthed, in the doorway. Andrew crossed the road and scrabbled at the driver's side door. It seemed to be locked. "Margaret! Margaret! Stop!" he shouted and hammered at her window.

Margaret hit the gas. Andrew staggered to one side, lost his balance and fell heavily onto the road.

Markie ran forward as Margaret hit the pillar again. It snapped, and the car hit the side of the house. Its engine died. Later, Gerry was to bless the house's ancient stone foundation which was all that kept the car from driving into the dining room.

Markie reached Andrew as a shocked Gerry crept cautiously out of the front door. Andrew was half-sitting up, examining a grazed elbow. Markie knelt on the road and embraced him. "Andy, are you okay?" Gerry turned her attention to Margaret. She was slumped in the car.

"Oh, my God," Gerry mumbled and ran toward her. Andrew followed.

Markie directed traffic. The faces of astonished drivers peered at the drama as they edged around the debris on the road.

"God, I hope no one calls the police," Andrew muttered as he neared the car.

"She may need an ambulance, Andrew!" Gerry said angrily.

The driver's door opened. Margaret stepped out, smiling and triumphant. She appeared to be drunk. "Enjoy your housh, Gerry," she slurred. Then she fell into a juniper bush.

"Get her in the house! Get her in the house!" Andrew said urgently as more gawkers drove by.

"Are you kidding me?" Gerry began. "She'll sabotage the inside!"

"Please, Gerry! Just help me!" Between them they lifted Margaret and brought her to the front door. Markie was picking up fragments from the road and tossing them into Gerry's driveway.

"Good grief!" Gerry said, looking over her shoulder as they staggered into the foyer, itself half-filled with odds and ends from the shed. "What a mess!"

The cats agitated around their feet as they supported Margaret into the living room and plopped her in a chair. "Coffee?" Andrew suggested.

Cats, disturbed by the assault on their home and seeking Gerry's nearness, followed her into the kitchen. Andrew heard a loud, "Oh, my God!" and then silence. The kitchen door slammed and he heard the extended sound of running water. He looked at Margaret. She appeared to be asleep, head lolling, her breathing heavy.

The kitchen door opened just a bit and Gerry's arm holding a cat appeared. She plopped the cat in the living room and closed the door. The process was repeated a half dozen times. Andrew noticed the cats' feet leaving little wet prints on the wooden floor. There was a strong smell of dill pickles. Despite the situation, or because of it, he giggled.

"And they ate my lunch!" Gerry said in exasperation as she finally exited the kitchen. She handed him a mug of coffee and a glass of water. "Better try offering the water first, don't you think?"

While Andrew gave Margaret sips of water, Gerry caught glimpses of Markie going back and forth in the front driveway. Gerry opened a front window and stuck her head out. "Thanks, Markie."

Markie was sweeping the driveway. She winked at Gerry. "Never a dull moment."

Gerry sighed and drew her head back in.

"Thanks for not calling the police," Andrew said softly. Margaret was more awake and he was holding the coffee as she drank.

She shuddered at the taste. "Shweet!" she said.

Gerry smiled. Good. She'd added the sugar to counteract shock. Margaret probably took her coffee unsweetened to stay slim. The bit — Gerry's eyes widened as she bent over her cousin. "Margaret, did you egg my house? And spray-paint it?"

Andrew looked at Gerry with astonishment. "When was this?"

"Easter Monday. While I was at yours." Again she addressed Margaret. "I saw the car, Margaret. Did you do it?"

Margaret opened one eye and squinted at Gerry. She grinned maliciously. "I'll never tell."

Andrew lost his patience. "Margaret! What do you think you're doing!? Do you want to go back to the institution? Is that what you want?"

Gerry ignored him. She brought her lips close to Margaret's ear. "And what if I tell, eh, Margaret? What if I tell what I know?"

Margaret's eyes became slits. Then, to Gerry's astonishment, they filled with tears. "Wanna go home!" Margaret wailed. "Want Mummy!"

Gerry recoiled. Andrew soothed. "All right, Margaret. I'll take you home. Please, please, Gerry, don't make a complaint. I'll pay for everything. Just let me take Margaret home to Mother and I'll come back and help you clean up. Please?"

Gerry looked at him. She thought he was making a mistake. She looked at Margaret, more to be pitied than anything. "All right," she reluctantly agreed. "But you don't need to come back. Markie already cleaned up and I need a break." Only the cats saw Margaret's sly look of satisfaction as Andrew led her away.

Doug returned to a quiet scene of disaster. Gerry had dragged an old chair over to the parking pad and turned her back on it all, was looking at the lake, drinking coffee.

He rushed to where she sat. "Are you all right? Was anyone hurt?"

"Do you recognize the car, Doug?" She accompanied him to the front of the house.

"It's Mary's." He seemed stupefied. "Did one of the boys do this?" She shook her head and he relaxed — a bit. "Mary?" She negated that guess as well. "Ah." He lapsed into silence. "Margaret, I suppose." She nodded. He sighed and she saw him shut down. "I bought us subs. Do you want yours?" he asked quietly.

She nodded and threw her arms around him. "We're okay, Doug. We're okay. No matter what Margaret does. Believe it." She held his face in her hands and kissed him.

"I'll get the sandwiches and you can tell me all about it."

Their quiet afternoon of doing a little painting and furniture cleaning morphed into driving to a friend of Doug's to pick up a truck, to the hardware store for lumber, and then to the tool rental company for a temporary brace for the front entranceway roof. If it hadn't been for her nagging worry about what Margaret might do next, Gerry might have almost enjoyed riding around with Doug.

When they got home, Mary's car was gone. Andrew must have either driven it or had it towed away. Doug examined the house wall. "Look at that," he said admiringly. "The foundation took the hit. All that happened to the siding was a scratch in the wood and some paint scraped off. Get that done today and paint the back wall. You can carry on with the furniture, what's left of it."

They examined the pile of broken bits Markie had assembled. "Looks like I lost a bureau, a lamp, a rake and a chair," Gerry said.

"Save the wood for kindling. It's not so bad. There are lots of things left. They'll make for a great spring sale in a few weeks. You'll see. The pickers and garage salers will descend on this stuff."

They worked until supper. "I've got to go," he said regretfully. "I don't like leaving you."

Gerry looked at Andrew's house. His car was gone. She spoke grimly. "I think I'll be safe tonight, anyway. Right at this moment

Andrew is probably ranting to Aunt Mary about how she can't leave Margaret unsupervised. Maybe he'll sleep over there tonight."

"Hardly with Markie," murmured Doug.

Gerry reddened, but more in anger than embarrassment. "I'd forgotten about my aunt's views. Maybe Markie will sleep at Cathy's, if she's not welcome at Aunt Mary's. Anyway, I'll be fine. I've got my early warning system." She gestured at the cats, many of whom had joined them in the living room. "And my attack cat." She pointed at Bob.

Doug hugged her. "That's good to know. But call me, eh? If anything happens?"

"I will."

After he left, Gerry grew pensive. She made a cup of tea and picked up the phone.

Prudence sounded tired but calm. "Thank you for calling. Did you and Doug get everything done that you wanted to today?"

"Em. Yes. Pretty much." Prudence had enough to think about without hearing about Margaret's rampage. "Er. I wondered if you needed anything. Groceries? A meal?"

"Thanks, but no. Rita brought me a plate about an hour ago and I have food in the house."

Gerry was at a loss. "Prudence, I just want to say — "

"I went to identify him," Prudence said dreamily. "In the hospital morgue."

Gerry caught her breath. "Oh, God, I should have — "

"No, no. Rita and Charlie took me. It was good to be with them." She laughed weakly. "They were bickering as usual. It was good to be around normal people."

"You're normal, Prudence."

"Oh, I know. But the circumstances — aren't."

There was a pause. "Do you need a drive anywhere tomorrow?"

"No. I'll just make the arrangements by phone. Anyway, I can't really make them until the police release the — the body. It's foul play, they say."

"Foul play?" Gerry felt like she was in an Agatha Christie TV drama.

"You know. Murder."

14

When Doug and the Hudsons arrived early Friday morning, Gerry thought she'd be able to work while they made their repairs. She was woefully behind in her *Mug the Bug* comic strip. So much had been happening, she only had one week's worth prepared.

The previous night, after speaking with Prudence, she'd called Cathy and been invited to dinner with her and Markie. Cathy had made moussaka, oven-roasted lemon potatoes and herbed rice with chocolate layer cake for dessert. Gerry had listened to Markie and Cathy's quiet conversation and been soothed.

Now the shouts of the Hudsons, and Doug's quieter responses, combined with the sounds of banging and drilling, as well as the occasional *beep beep beep* as, for some reason, the Hudsons found it necessary to repeatedly back up one of their trucks, made work impossible.

She loaded the Mini with a box of books, and cat carriers with Jay and Winnie in one, Frank and Joe in the other, and carefully backed onto Main Road, leaving the chaos behind. She breathed a sigh of relief. If the cats were amenable, she planned to stay away from her house as long as possible.

She drove for almost an hour to a pet shelter new to her. They let her leave ten books. She worked her way back to Lovering, sometimes dropping in somewhere she'd already been, or somewhere new, like a children's bookstore she'd heard of. There she was enthusiastically received by the owner who immediately signed her up for a Saturday morning book-signing in a few weeks.

After this interview, the cats began to mew when she returned to the car, so she headed for Lovering. Remarkably, the vets were running on time. All Jay needed were her stitches removed and the boys were quickly checked and inoculated.

"Nice healthy cats," Dr. Perry complimented her.

"Thanks." She remembered the painting she was supposed to do of his old dog, and edged out the door of the examining room. "Have you got some, er, papers for me, possibly in an envelope, from Dr. Morin?" she asked the receptionist in a low voice. Dr. Perry was standing with his back to them, looking at the next patient's file.

The receptionist rummaged for a large brown envelope. "Here you are," she said brightly. "Oh. We sold half the copies of your book. Here's the money." She handed Gerry $100.

Dr. Perry quipped, "That makes a change, eh? Leaving the vets with money in your pocket?"

"Don't worry," Gerry joked back, leaving the cash on the counter. "It's coming right back to you." She paid the difference and took her little group home.

All was quiet. The Hudsons and Doug were sitting at the picnic table on the back lawn. Doug put out his cigarette and got up to greet her. "I hope you don't mind. I made us all a coffee. I could only find the Belgian chocolate one." He made a face only Gerry could see. Doug liked his coffee strong and plain.

"And very nice, too," the older Hudson said, raising his mug politely. "Got to get some of that for the missus."

Gerry inspected their work. The jack was gone from under the entranceway roof and a new wooden pillar was installed. The roof of the shed had been repaired as well as the broken window.

"Just got to fix the shed floor this aft, and we're done," Doug said.

"Thank you all very much," Gerry said loudly, to include the Hudsons as well. They smiled and nodded. She went inside and released the four cats. They all ran towards the downstairs toilet where the seven cat litter boxes were kept. "Sorry, guys," she called after them. "I won't do that again."

After lunch she was able to concentrate, and got one *Mug* strip done and another roughed out. She opened the envelope and looked at the photos of Dr. Perry's dog, Merlin. "What a love," she murmured, looking at the tongue hanging out under the white muzzle, the reddish-brown fur whitened by age around the patient eyes and floppy ears. She sighed. "Dogs are so — nice." A simple portrait, she decided, the dog looking at the viewer.

The Hudsons' trucks beeping backwards announced their departures. She found Doug in the shed, sweeping. "Why, it's quite a large space when it's not full of stuff," she noted.

"Make a great workshop," he suggested.

"Or a shop," Gerry said. "It could just be open on the weekends during the mild weather. A place to sell my artwork."

"Yee-es," Doug said doubtfully. "But do you really want another job?"

"I could work in the house at my freelance stuff and just come out here when a car stopped."

"See how you like selling when we have your spring garage sale. Then decide."

Gerry paused as she remembered how exhausting sitting in the mall with the CRAS people had been. "Hm. You may have something there. Plus, I'd have to stay in all weekend. Might not be so much fun. Anyway, we need a place for the wheelbarrow, lawnmower, and all the other tools, no?"

He nodded. "And next winter's wood, don't forget. I've got to leave. Working at the legion tonight and the yacht club tomorrow. From barkeep to boat-mender," he quipped. He hugged and kissed her. "Be careful, eh?"

"I will." With regret, she watched him go. She wondered if Mary was going ahead with her plan to sell Margaret and Doug's house. Would he be willing to come live with her at The Maples? Did she even want that? And what about his sons?

She made a coffee and, for the first time that spring, sat in her screened back porch and watched the birds.

The people walked out of the lake and stood on the lawn. The ones in the front few rows were solid, their features visible. A little behind them were less substantial figures, their clothes a bit more old-fashioned, their features a little less distinct.

The people farthest in the back had little form; neither were they standing. Oh, they were upright, but it was as if details like feet or hands or facial expressions were unimportant. They hovered behind the more solid presences.

There were a lot more people this time. More men: in overalls and work caps, or old-fashioned suits and hats. Some sported gloves and canes and looked prosperous. Others stared dumbly ahead, their clothes stained and torn, their faces blank, expecting nothing.

And, in the front row, stood two little girls who looked somewhat like each other. The little girls had linked hands. They wore the same dresses. Their free hands pointed straight ahead.

Gerry woke with a start. Her jaw jerked down and she took a deep shuddering breath. She lay on her back, eyes open. Still night. What had woken her? A desire to escape the dream? She hadn't been afraid exactly, more a witness than a participant. Yet it had felt as though the two little girls were looking right at her.

The cats on the bed were unfazed. Bob, Seymour, Jay and Lightning slumbered, each in their own little zone. I need a bigger bed, she thought, and wondered what it would be like to wake up with Doug by her side all the time. He'd say it was just a dream and I should go back to sleep. She turned on her side.

A curious sound close to the front of the house brought her to full consciousness. She went to the window in her room, which overlooked the main road, and looked down. If anyone was there, they'd be hidden by the porch roof.

She turned to look at her clock radio. 12:34 gleamed red. She remembered the last time the clock had displayed those numbers, the night Jay seemed possessed. She shivered and put on her robe. She always found it slightly creepy when the numbers all lined up like that when she just happened to observe them. 11:11 was worse for some reason. "You're being fanciful," she said aloud. The sound was repeated. Jay woke up.

Remembering how demented Jay had become the last time she'd been up at night, Gerry quickly picked her up and held her firmly. "No climbing the curtains tonight, please, Miss Jay." The little face turned upward and the little eyes opened wide. "Oh, right. Miss Innocent," Gerry said and snuggled her face into the kitten's soft fur.

This time, the sound, a kind of *thock, thock*, seemed to come from the side of the house nearest to Blaise's. Gerry moved to that window and peeked out the edge of one curtain.

The bare apple tree below a sliver of moon. Some stars. The lawn dark instead of white. In the perennial garden the beginning of new growth. The cat struggled in her arms.

Thocka, thocka, thocka. Now coming from the back of the house. Could it be a bird? Trying to get in? She'd had blue jays hammering periodically at her siding for insects. They made a similar sound. Perhaps one of those giant woodpeckers? But most birds rested at night, didn't they? Was it bats?

She cautiously moved into the bedroom formerly occupied by Aunt Maggie, where four of the cats still liked to sleep, preserving some memory of their lost mistress, or perhaps just because they were creatures of habit.

Whatever the *thock* was, it hadn't woken the Honour Guard. Blackie, Whitey, Mouse and Runt were curled up on the bed's comforter, though they blinked sleepily as Gerry entered with Jay. She edged to the room's back window and looked out.

A haze hung over the lake, a thin patchy mist that eddied slightly. The water was calm.

Jay wrenched free and ran out of the room. Gerry followed her downstairs. She wondered why she wasn't more afraid.

The sounds led them along the back of the house, from the bamboo room, still shut for the winter and colder than the rest of the house, to the dining room where more cats slumbered then woke, as Jay agitated around two of the chairs, rearing on her hind legs and clawing at the upholstery. Gerry was briefly distracted but more sounds made her run into her little art gallery, adjacent to the dining room, then into the living room. Every time she looked out a window, there was only the peaceful early spring landscape and the *thock* had stopped.

Jay followed her into the living room, this time pawing at the two rocking chairs before skittering into the kitchen where she hopped onto the counter, straining to look out the window that faced the shed. Gerry looked too.

The sounds were very near. Gerry unlocked the side door and stepped onto the little kitchen porch, knowing the outer door was locked.

A face reared out of the darkness. A face wearing a mask. The mask of classical tragedy, the downturned mouth and weeping eyes frozen forever in a painful grimace.

One part of Gerry's mind said this couldn't be happening even as the other part assured her it was.

The figure's arm came up and it directed a stream of red fluid at the glass. Gerry screamed and the figure ducked out of sight. She stepped back, hitting the door frame with her elbow as she retreated into the kitchen, slammed the door and locked it.

She sank onto the floor, holding her funny bone and breathing heavily. Jay jumped off the counter and onto her lap, purring and kneading her chest. "Jay, listen." The kitten stopped purring. There were no more thocking sounds. The house was quiet. The stovetop clock face showed 12:38. The whole episode had taken only four minutes!

Gerry felt her heartbeat slow. But she was still frightened. She slid up the wall and reached for the phone. She jerked as a mousetrap snapped.

"I got here as quick as I could," Doug said as she let him in the front door. She didn't want to go near the side door. "You've been tagged again, I'm afraid." He stepped aside, pulling her out onto the front stoup. On the door someone had spray-painted a big red X.

"This is getting old," Gerry said wearily. She slipped on a pair of rubber boots and they walked around to the garden side of the house. Four letters defaced the wall. WE'RE. Gerry ran around the back. Eight letters sent a chill down her back. WATCHING. She backed away from the house, revolted.

Doug grabbed her hand. They continued around to the parking pad. Her side door was awash in red paint. "That explains the *thocka thocka* sound. You know — when you shake a can of spray paint?" She inspected the red and white Mini and attempted a weak laugh. "At least they left the car alone. Probably thought it was red enough. Come inside, Doug. Oh, I forgot about the boys. Can you stay?"

"James is in Montreal. I peeked in at Geoff and David — sound asleep. They'll be fine."

As long as Margaret's not on the loose, Gerry couldn't help thinking. "I'll make tea," is what she said. And, "Oh, I forgot." She removed the sad remains in the trap under the sink and dropped both into the garbage.

As they waited for the kettle to boil, they looked at Jay, sitting on the counter. "She's the only one who bothered to get up while all this was going on. The rest stayed asleep. So much for my early warning system."

"Kittens are hyper, though. I know I'm sometimes woken up by Didi flipping some object around. What was it yesterday? Oh yes, an empty toilet paper tube in the bathtub. She was rolling around after that thing like a snowboarder on a halfpipe. And when I took it away so I could get some sleep, she went up the shower curtain. That reminds me. I need a new shower curtain."

Gerry laughed. The kettle boiled. They took the tea to bed.

As usual, Doug was gone when Gerry woke. She stretched luxuriously, then remembered the mess on her house. "Damn!" She sat up and hurriedly dressed. "Cat breakfasts, cat boxes, phone Jean and say I'll be late, phone tool rental and see when they open." Cats done, she made a coffee while she found the phone numbers. "Jean? Sorry to call so early. Listen. I'm going to be late for the event. In fact, don't be surprised if I don't make it at all. What? No, I'm fine. It's a bit of emergency home maintenance. No. He's fine. He's fit in perfectly. He's a nice cat. Okay. Thanks."

She blessed the god of handymen and women as the recorded message informed her the rental shop would open at eight. "Bye, cats! I'll be home in a jiffy."

By 8:30 she was fiddling with the power washer and by 11:00 she again had a house free of hideous red accents. She changed, put the machine in her car, grabbed some of her books and was off. She'd return the machine and eat at the mall.

Today CRAS's rehoming operation was set up in a mall outside the entrance to a large pet supplies store. Miriam and Heather, Jean, and a mostly fresh crop of kittens and some of the same adult cats who'd been there last time were hard at work when Gerry arrived.

"Oh, good," Jean said. "I just sold the last copy we had of your book."

Many cat-related conversations and several hours later, as she was sipping a tea Jean had treated the crew to, Gerry realized an old man who'd earlier engaged Heather in chat about one of the adult cats had been sitting on a bench staring at them for hours. "Is he one of the regulars?" she asked Heather.

Heather gave the man a quick glance. "No. Apart from today, I've never seen him before. Do you know him?"

Gerry shook her head and returned to her position among the cage-topped tables. Today she was on kittens and they were infinitely easier to work with than the dignified adult cats. They couldn't help but do adorable things when people stopped to observe. Half the time she put one in someone's arms, they adopted it.

As she modelled one kitten, letting it climb around her neck and shoulders, much to the delight of a few children gathered near, she kept glancing at the old man. Did she know him?

He was old but not really old. His regular features and hair hinted he might once have been handsome. Medium weight, little pot-belly, smoker. She knew the latter fact because every little while he would pat his pocket, extract a cigarette, put it between his lips and walk to the nearest exit. He must have been taking only a few puffs each time because he'd be back on his bench a minute later

I wonder, she thought, and went for a pee the next time he went out for a smoke. But instead of going to the bathroom, she turned down a hallway of the mall and loitered, pretending to look in a shoe store window. She didn't have long to wait.

The man, huffing and puffing, walked right by her, caught sight of her and drew back slightly in surprise. He kept walking. Gerry's narrowed gaze followed his progress out of sight. She returned to CRAS's display.

When she loaded her remaining books in the Mini at the end of the day, she looked carefully around before getting behind the wheel. She took a deep breath. Last night and now this. She checked the rear-view mirror all the way home.

15

Sunday morning, just as she was sitting down to a late mega-breakfast of kippers, scrambled eggs, buttered toast and Earl Grey tea, her phone rang. Cursing, she rose to answer it. A sad quiet voice said, "Hello, Gerry."

"Prudence? Is that you?"

"Gerry, can you come over? There's something I want to show you."

"Of course! I'm glad to hear from you. I'll just bolt my food and be right there."

When Gerry arrived at Prudence's, a few neighbours stood in the driveway with Prudence. "You just missed the police," Prudence said wearily.

"Why? What happened? Are you hurt?" Prudence pointed at the house.

The window boxes with their cheerful faux red tulips had been wrenched from the wall and smashed. The front door window had likewise been broken. "I was at church," she said.

"Anyone with a piece of wood or a rock could have done it," one of the neighbours said.

"Did anyone see anything?" Gerry asked.

The man continued, "I saw a white compact drive away. Two men in it, I think."

"Men?" Gerry pushed. "Not boys?"

The neighbour frowned. "Men, boys. What difference does it make?"

"The police took the message," Prudence said.

"Let's go inside," Gerry suggested. The neighbours walked away. "What message?"

They stepped over broken glass in the tiny entranceway. "What message?" Gerry repeated, closing the interior door. At least there was an interior door, though it was lockless. "We have to get that window repaired, Prudence. It's still too cold at night and the door's not secure."

"A glazier who makes house calls on Sundays? I'd like to meet one of those," Prudence managed with a return of her usual sardonic humour. "Coffee?"

"Please. Prudence, my house was tagged again Friday night, and I saw the perpetrator. But he was wearing a mask."

"How frightening. My neighbour didn't say if the guys in the car had masks on."

"Well, they'd take them off once they got in the car, right?"

"Maybe." She brought two coffees to the kitchen table and sat down heavily. "I'm too old for all this drama."

"What did the message say?"

"Oh. It was on a crumpled-up piece of paper they threw inside after they broke the window. It said 'Where is it?'"

"It?"

"It."

"Wait a minute." Gerry thought. "Both our houses vandalized in the same weekend. Are they connected? What connects us?"

"Lots of stuff. Family relationships, your house. You've hardly ever been here."

"No and yes. What connects the two vandalizations? Is that a word?"

Prudence clarified. "Vandalism is probably the word you're thinking of. When damage is random. Otherwise, vandalization is correct."

Gerry looked at her in admiration. "Really, Prudence? Time for grammar? And you know the answer?"

Prudence shrugged. "Well, you asked."

Gerry continued. "Where was I? Oh, yes. What connects us — our two houses — is you. You go to both places regularly."

"Right. But maybe your house was done because of something you've done and mine was done because of something completely different. No connection."

"What did the police think?"

"At first they said kids but when I mentioned my late husband had just been released from prison and murdered, their ears pricked up."

"God, Prudence, I'm sorry. I'd forgotten all about Alex. I guess he's just not very real to me. In life or death."

They drank their coffee.

Prudence broke the silence. "Your house — was it bad words like last time?"

"A big X on the front door, then 'We're watching' in capital letters all along one side and the back. And red paint on the side door glass. I cleaned it up yesterday morning. Now there's even more painting to be done."

Prudence tsk-tsked. "Hours of work. If it is connected to Alex, I'm sorry, Gerry. Even when he's dead, nothing but trouble." She sounded bitter.

"Don't say that, Prudence. There must have been something good about him. And even if there wasn't, much, it's bad for you to be so negative."

Prudence sighed. "I know. I have to let it go. Maybe after the funeral."

"When is it?"

"Next Thursday."

"I'll be there."

When Gerry left, Prudence was phoning for someone to come repair her door. Gerry decided, if she got tagged again, it would be pointless to clean the graffiti off her house — until she knew who was doing it and why. They'd just return and do it again.

She spent the afternoon making a start on the painting of Dr. Perry's dog. Around seven she received a peculiar invitation.

Gerry cursed as she guided the Mini towards downtown Montreal. What had she been thinking, agreeing to meet at nine o'clock on a Monday morning? It felt like everyone in the world wanted to go where she was headed.

She drummed her fingers on the steering wheel, waiting for the car ahead of her to move. She'd been going up this ramp for twenty minutes! She grinned. Probably a wild goose chase anyway. With a couple of characters.

The characters were waiting in the lobby of Marion's old building when a flustered and sweaty Gerry finally arrived. Bertie bobbed out the front door, waved and bobbed back in. Gerry switched on the car's flashers. A taxi almost took off her side mirror edging around the Mini. Other cars behind her honked.

Bertie reappeared, giving an arm to Marion. She was dressed the way she had been when they'd met at Frey's: in a wine red turban, fur coat and pearls. The only difference was that today's was a short fur coat. It looked like mink and when Bertie handed her into the front seat, Gerry caught a familiar whiff of mothballs and perfume. He clambered into the back.

"And we're off!" Gerry said, engaging the clutch. "Sorry I'm late. Too much traffic."

"Difficult city to penetrate during rush hour, I'm told," came from behind her. Bertie sniffed. "Of course, I don't drive. Never needed to."

"I can drive," chirped Marion. "We used to motor out to the country every weekend when I was a girl. Father taught me. I don't have a licence though."

Bertie muttered, "Why am I not surprised?"

Marion ignored him and directed Gerry. "Turn right here."

Gerry turned into the lane that ran alongside Marion's building. A garbage truck blocked the way. "Damn," said Marion. "You'll have to back up."

A perspiring Gerry carefully backed up, avoiding pedestrians on the sidewalk as well as oncoming traffic. "Well, this is fun," remarked Bertie brightly.

She glared at him in the mirror. "Do either of you know where we're going or how to get there?" she asked in what she hoped were neutral tones.

Marion removed a map from her purse with a flourish. "Of course I know. You just drive. I'll be the navigator. Now where are my glasses?" She rummaged in her purse. This time, when Gerry met Bertie's amused gaze in the mirror, she smiled back.

Forty-five minutes later they'd extricated themselves from Montreal and were heading north towards the Laurentian Mountains. At first the land was flat with sprawling small towns and suburbs along the highway. Not inspiring.

They veered left and the mountains began. Gerry, used to the Ottawa River valley's relatively mountain-free views, was awed by the towering peaks. They passed St. Sauveur and Ste. Adèle. Gerry would have looked more but the winding and hilly road demanded her attention.

"Next exit," cautioned Marion. "There. Val-David. Okay, when we get to the town, we look for rue de l'Église. On your right. That's your job, Bertie. By the time I can read street signs, I'm usually past them."

They were now on a two-lane secondary highway. Val-David was a few businesses and houses either side of the road. "There!"

said Bertie. Gerry turned right and began to understand why people would want to live here.

Small houses of varying styles and ages stood on large treed lots. The road twisted and she realized they were on the side of a hill, caught glimpses of a lake down below to her right. They came to a stop sign and Marion dithered. "I think we turn right. Turn right." They descended the slope to where the lake shone in the sun. "Park here."

"But there aren't any houses on this road," Bertie protested.

"Look across the lake, you simp. That's the house. Anyway, we don't want to get too close. We're here to observe." She returned the map and reading glasses to her purse and stared across the water. Bertie got out and leaned on the car, smoking his pipe.

The house at the far end of the lake was modern and lovely, a series of stacked and attached A-frames. The fact that the top of each 'A' was rounded gave it a softness of form. Made of glass and golden-stained wood, it blended remarkably well with the mostly coniferous surrounding trees. It also looked remarkably expensive. And new.

"Gossip is," Bertie began, "that that's where his wife caught them. At the 'cottage'—if you can call it that."

"She took the city house—a nice old stone pile in Westmount—and he got this. And his mistress, of course." Marion sounded unfazed by this behaviour.

"And this was about five or six years ago?" Gerry asked.

Marion nodded. "The Freys had just finished building the cottage. I suppose he might have begun stealing before the girlfriend appeared. Maybe he found he couldn't afford the cottage once it was finished."

"It must have cost millions," Bertie agreed. "And now he's paying to support two households plus the wife's alimony settlement as well. He's got the motive."

Gerry thought of nice Mr. Frey, portly, in late middle age, falling in love, struggling financially, then betraying the trust of his customers and his family's traditions. She sighed. "How on earth do you propose to prove it? If it's true."

"Well, really," expostulated Marion. "Who else could it have been?"

"What about Ms. Adams?" Gerry suggested.

"Her?" Marion spoke with scorn. "She's so straight, she probably faints at the sight of a paperclip."

"They're called trombones in French," Bertie offered dreamily. "Did you know that?"

"I did not," replied Gerry. "Cute."

"We're drifting off topic," snapped Marion. "Everyone is searched coming in and out of Frey's. Who wouldn't be searched? The owner, of course. He pays for the security! We'll confront him. He's weak. Was always weak. I knew his mother."

"You knew everyone's mother," Bertie muttered.

Gerry smothered a giggle. She coughed instead.

"What? What?" demanded Marion.

"You didn't know my mother," Bertie replied sweetly. "Because she didn't emigrate from her Liverpool slum until the 1950s. She only got as far as Saint-Henri. She never made it to Westmount."

Marion glared but said nothing.

"Look." Gerry pointed to one of the many decks on the beautiful house. A woman had stepped out onto the deck holding a mug. She looked across the lake, seemingly right at them.

"She's not young and blonde," Gerry said in a disappointed sounding voice.

"No," said Marion. "She's a perfectly nice woman from the Freys' circle of friends, a widow. She's far nicer than Mrs. Frey. I don't blame him. But he can't steal from his own clients. No. We'll confront him."

"Is he there today?" Gerry asked.

"Drive by the house and we'll look at their cars. Bertie, hop in!"

Bertie hopped and Gerry drove up the slope, turning right along a dirt road. As they passed Frey's chalet, she slowed.

"Three cars. He must be there," Bertie said.

"Wait! Wait!" Gerry said and increased speed to pass the house. "Do we really want to confront him in front of his friend? What if she doesn't know?" She parked again.

Marion gave her a look. "You're being very considerate of someone who may have robbed you of hundreds of thousands of dollars."

"One: he may be innocent. Two: do we want him to go to jail or are we just happy if he repays the money to the other clients and returns my Borduas?"

"I don't really want to involve the police," Bertie said slowly. "We'd have to go to court and that would be boring and time consuming. You don't want to go to court, do you, Marion?"

"Certainly not! But he's got to make restitution. How will he do that?"

"He'll have to sell his lovely house," Gerry said sadly.

"All right. We'll confront him in Montreal. At Frey's. Or maybe I can invite him to appraise something of mine at my apartment. Now, I know a marvellous place for lunch on the way home. Where's that map? My glasses..."

Gerry and Bertie exchanged a look in the mirror. Bertie stiffly saluted and this time Gerry laughed.

Lunch was fabulous, at a French country inn in the next village, also by a lake and with incredible views of the surrounding mountainsides. They ate trout. Marion ordered a bottle of wine, most of which she drank. She snored on the drive home while Gerry and Bertie conversed quietly.

He decanted the sleepy lady in front of her building. "I'm afraid it's rush hour, again, Gerry. Take care."

It had been a long day. When she got home and after she'd attended to the cats, she checked her phone answering machine.

Bea had called. It could wait. She went to bed early and slept without dreaming.

"The For Sale sign is up," Doug said grimly. He'd dropped by for lunch and was helping Gerry carry the furniture stored in her foyer back into the shed. They were trying to arrange it nicely so it could all be seen when Gerry had her sale.

"Oh, Doug, I'm so sorry. What do the boys say?"

"Not much. I told them to make up their own minds and think about what's best for all of them. To be honest, I think David dislikes Mary. He said he wanted to stay with me."

"So that leaves James and Geoff," Gerry mused, already counting bedrooms in case they all moved in with her. It made her nervous just thinking about it.

"I wouldn't be surprised if James just moves to Montreal. He couch surfs there anyway during the week so he can avoid the commute for school. On public transit it takes almost two hours."

"That's understandable," Gerry said, thinking of her adventures driving into and out of the city.

"As for Geoff, I'm not sure. He's the quietest of the three. The middle child. He might move in with Mary and Margaret. I just don't know. There. That's done it."

"It looks really nice. Thanks, Doug. You working today?"

"Yeah. New garden to dig. Gotta go." He kissed her. "Love you."

"Love you too," she said thoughtfully and watched him leave.

It was an overcast day and she shivered as she let herself back into the house. She got out the vacuum cleaner and tidied up the foyer. She felt warmer. "But it would still be nice to make a fire, eh, cats? It might be one of the last ones until next fall. Cats? Cats?"

The cats, as usual shocked into invisibility by the infernal racket of the ancient vacuum, began to reappear.

Gerry made a fire and settled down to work on her dog portrait. She could sure use the 500 bucks, what with paying the

Hudsons and Doug for the shed and other repairs and renting the power washer—twice! And three or four more cats should go to the vets this Friday. It would be good if she could finish the painting this week. She buckled down to work, stopping only to feed the cats, tend the fire, and make coffee.

Trying to save money—all those vet bills!—she did not order a pizza, though her hand reached for the phone when she got hungry. Instead she had baked beans and toast and a glass of milk. She looked at the plate and added some lettuce and half a tomato. "There. All the food groups. I think. I think beans equal meat." The cats looked doubtful.

Gerry knew she should be working on *Mug the Bug*. Or planning tomorrow's art lesson. Or thinking about what to serve her students at their next class. But the sheer pleasure of creation was upon her. She finished the portrait of the old dog Merlin late that evening and for the second night in a row fell into dreamless sleep.

She slept in. For once, when she needed them to, the cats failed to rouse her. It was ten when Jay finally painfully tromped on her hair close to its roots and tickled her eyes with her whiskers. Gerry saw the time. "Argh!" Prudence wasn't coming, what with getting her house repaired and planning Alex's funeral. Gerry was on her own.

"Okay, don't panic. It's just a few people coming for a drawing lesson. They won't care if the dining room chairs are hairy. Focus on the living room. Thank goodness I vacuumed the foyer yesterday!" All this was said to Bob, Seymour and Jay after she dashed to the bathroom for a quick wash, then brushed her hair in her bedroom. Lightning, disturbed by Gerry's sudden energy, was long gone.

The cats were fed in record time. A large coffee was prepared in Gerry's travel mug so it could accompany her as she worked. By eleven the place looked tidy.

"Argh!" she said again. "Now I'm supposed to bake?" She briefly contemplated driving to Lovering to buy something but decided it would be just as time-consuming as baking in the end.

She flipped through Aunt Maggie's recipe folder. Cinnamon buns! No time for yeast today but this recipe called for baking powder. She threw the dough together, made the yummy and very cinnamon-y filling, rolled out the dough into a rectangle, slapped on the filling, rolled up the dough, sliced the buns and got them into a buttered cupcake pan and then the oven in under twenty minutes. The kitchen was a mess but that didn't matter. She took a deep breath. Now what on earth was going to be the subject of today's lesson?

She stepped out onto the parking pad. Paranoia after recent events made her check that her car and both shed doors were locked. As she was turning away from the little door at the front of the shed, she saw the elderly man from the shopping centre drive by. He was in a compact white car and turned his head to look briefly at her, his face a blank.

In a daze she went into the house and sat down by the hearth. Slowly, she kindled a fire. The day was damp. The students would enjoy a fire. The oven timer dinged. She smelled hot dough and cinnamon as she lifted out the pan. She went to freshen up.

As she passed the convex mirror in the dining room, she looked at her face. It was as white as a ghost's.

PART 4

POUNCE

Kitten walked for the second time in her life on the back lawn. The day before, the girl had pushed aside a chest in the dining room and unpeeled tape from the edges of a small square of carpet tacked to the wall.

Kitten had been riveted when she saw other cats sniff at the square then shoulder their way through. A new cupboard! How delightful! She'd pushed and found herself outside.

That had been on a cool sunny afternoon. This was a wet early morning. Most of the other cats stayed inside when it was wet. But the world was such a novelty to Kitten, she couldn't resist.

For the most part, she stayed on the narrow decking along the back of the house, where there was some shelter from the raindrops. She dropped down onto a flagstone path. Now she was getting wet. Her ears pulled back and down in annoyance. Where — ? She sprinted to the picnic table and crouched underneath. Relatively dry. She swivelled her head and took in her surroundings.

House, car, shed, thicket, shore, lake. Lawn, pool, garden, trees, house. There were rustlings — so many! On the ground, in the trees, even in the air!

A shrew poked its nose out of one of its many burrow entranceways and exits. Kitten caught the movement and streaked toward it. The shrew dropped back into the ground. Kitten fixed her gaze on the hole for a moment. A noise from the shore diverted her.

A breeze rustled through dead grasses and bare foliage. It blew mist off the lake toward land.

Kitten blinked. From the mist, humans were beginning to take shape, becoming upright as the mist drew nearer, as though they'd been asleep and were now waking. Their forms began to detach and she could see individuals. Women shook their skirts into neatness, men straightened ties. Children were taken in hand by their mothers, their hair flattened, collars rearranged.

The shapes reached the shore and floated up onto the lawn. Kitten retreated back under the picnic table. The people lined up facing the house.

Two little girls at the centre of the first row held hands. They were similar to each other the way Kitten was similar to her littermates. One of the girls was much wispier than the other. That was the only difference.

The people gazed at the house but the little girls looked at Kitten. She felt her hairs tingle as they each pointed their free hand at her. They were smiling.

Perhaps she might —. She stood and tentatively walked out from under the table.

16

"So I thought instead of me setting a subject, we could have suggestions from you about what you'd like to draw, things you have difficulty with maybe?"

The students looked at each other. Christine went first. "Well, I have the most trouble with faces. Eyes, especially."

"Me too," chirped Ben. "My eyes always look insane." Judith giggled. "Not *my* eyes, Judy. What I'm drawing. They look like the googly eyes you can buy to stick on things."

Judith stopped giggling. "I would like to learn how to add a bit of colour to my sketches. Could we do that?"

"We can do both," Gerry said. "Sharon? June? Are you happy with those suggestions?"

Sharon huffed a bit. "I'm not comfortable drawing people. Not yet. I can't see them clearly. Not like I see a table or that stack of books, say."

Gerry suppressed a sigh. Anything with straight lines seemed to be Sharon's limit. She smiled. "But you would like to begin experimenting with colour?"

"I suppose," Sharon agreed grudgingly.

June nodded. "Whatever you suggest, Gerry," she whispered.

Gerry brought her coloured pencils from the closed-up studio in the bamboo room. Soon be back in here, she thought happily. "Turn to one of your old sketches and think about what colours would work to highlight what you've already done. Two or three would be a useful number to begin with. And you'll be doing more shading, though you can outline in colour too. Let's see what happens."

She herself took orange, black and white and flipped through her sketchbook to an old drawing of Marigold.

It was an approximation. She couldn't quite remember which eye was surrounded by orange and which by white fur, nor which white back leg had sported a big black spot. She did her best for ten minutes, built up the fire, then walked around making suggestions.

Sharon had ignored her instructions to limit herself to a few colours, but for once to good effect. She had previously sketched a quilt hanging on a wall and was making a good job of colouring the various squares in. Gerry gasped. "Sharon! This is lovely, did you make the quilt?" Sharon nodded, cheeks flushed with pride. Always praise if possible, Gerry the teacher reflected as she moved on to inspect Christine's work.

Both Christine and Judith were tinting portraits. Gerry made a few suggestions before looking at Ben's page. He'd drawn a few eyes and wasn't ready for colour. The eyes were indeed cock-eyed. "See?" he said helplessly.

"You know, Ben," she mused, "you could take what's a problem and turn it into something interesting. Think of Dali. Think of Picasso. Now look at your eyes again. Do you see what I'm talking about?" He nodded slowly. "Everything doesn't have to be representational." To show him what she meant, she got her own pad, flipped the page and quickly drew a deconstructed calico cat.

"I could never do something like that," he protested.

"Maybe. Maybe not. But try." She moved to where June sat, little Jay on her lap.

"Thank you for the mug," June said and showed her work. Obviously it was a recent sketch done at home. She'd meticulously copied the King Edward VIII mug and was now trying to tint it from memory. "If I get the colours wrong, I can always do it again.

Did you know he and his wife visited Hitler in Germany and were pro-Nazi?"

Gerry was taken aback. "How revolting! I didn't know. I wouldn't have bought the mug if I had."

"I don't mind. It's history. Maybe he regretted abdicating and having his brother take over. Maybe he thought Hitler would make him king again. If Germany won the war."

Gerry, whose grasp of high school twentieth-century European history had never been deep, paused. "Yes, well, you seem to have been very faithful to the original cup, as far as I can remember. Good job!" To be honest, Gerry was relieved not to be exposed to another one of June's spectral drawings. She went into the kitchen and prepared the snack.

She brought the food in on a tray. "I'm sorry, it's cinnamon buns again, but a different recipe."

Christine took a bun. "Oh, I know this recipe. I actually prefer these to the yeasted ones. Drier. More like a scone. Good with a cup of tea."

After their cinnamon buns and tea, the students were eager to keep working with colour; even Ben was persuaded to try. Gerry suggested which pencils they might want to buy and that they could even begin to think about charcoal and coloured chalks. The students left buzzing with anticipation.

As June stepped out the door, last as usual (Gerry couldn't help thinking her husband must enjoy his breaks from shepherding the ultra-shy June and sometimes delay picking her up.), she handed Gerry a four-by-six inch of paper. "I did it this morning at home," she whispered. "Maybe it will help."

Gerry looked down. The twins, Isabelle and Constance Catford, Prudence's aunt and mother, smiled up at her. They held hands. Their free hands pointed down at their feet where sat — black, white-tipped tail coiled around white feet, one of which displayed a distinctive black toe — the kitten, Jay.

Working on *Mug the Bug*'s adventures that evening calmed Gerry down. She was behind designing birthday cards featuring her tiny hero. As she was at a temporary loss for ideas, she focused on one relative at a time.

A card for fathers. She remembered the cards she'd made for her father when she'd been a child: coloured construction paper folded in half, decorated with crayoned drawings and glitter. And lots of X's and O's for kisses and hugs. Gerry had loved her father. Her brain slipped sideways.

Exes and woes. She thought of Doug and Margaret, Prudence and Alexander Crick. Woe aplenty.

She wondered if she could design a faux handmade card then scrapped the idea. "Brilliant, genius," she muttered. "Just what the card company wants you to suggest: that people make their own cards." She crumpled the paper and tossed it behind her.

A soft thud told her someone had risen to the challenge. She turned. Jay sat, batting the paper. Gerry picked up June's sketch.

Why would the woman pull a detail from a previous sketch and then include in it a cat she'd been seeing for the last few months? Gerry, who knew how creative minds worked, could rationalize June's sketch. But. Something else was going on. She examined the drawing more carefully.

There was no background, just a thin strip of green on which the three figures rested. One of the twins was noticeably thinner than the other; her cheekbones and the tendons in her neck visible. Isabelle, perhaps? The one who died young? They both had a look of Prudence.

Gerry sighed. A card for a father. She pictured hers in a recliner watching sports on TV. She drew Mug's father in a similar posture. She put a sports banner in one hand and a canned beverage in the other. Words, words. "I've got it!" she exclaimed and wrote, "To the biggest fan!" on the front of the card below the father, and "From your biggest fan!" inside. There she drew Mug jumping up and down in a bleacher, dangerously close to human feet in sneakers.

"That'll have to do," she sighed, feeling the card wasn't up to her usual standards. She'd try again another day.

When she revisited the card over coffee the next morning, it didn't seem so bad. She even had time to do a rough draft of a card for grandmothers. "To a super Grandma!" it read on the front with a drawing of Mug painfully trying to drag a full-sized box of chocolates toward his diminutive relative waiting in a rocking chair.

Inside the card the words had changed, but only slightly. They now read, "To Super Grandma!" and the sedentary little figure from the front picture had acquired a tiny fluttering cape and was supporting the chocolate box with one finger while a panting and prostrate Mug admired from the floor. Silly stuff but it was her and Mug's brand. She sat back, satisfied. Now that she had the daily strip and the cards, she wondered if she could create a desk calendar starring Mug. She could cannibalize her strips. Or maybe a book. That wouldn't be too hard to do. Just collect old cartoons. She shook herself. "Like I don't already have enough to do," she observed to Mother, who was grooming Jay on the hearth rug. Mother paused. "We women do what we have to," she seemed to say. Jay scooted away. Gerry changed into black slacks and sweater and drove to the Catholic church for Alex Crick's funeral.

There were quite a few people, which surprised her. Bea and Cece waved but she spotted Lucy Hanlan, a close friend of Prudence's, sitting alone and, after a few words with her friends, joined Lucy in a pew. The Catholic liturgy was going to be unfamiliar to Gerry and she whispered in Lucy's ear, "Tell me when to get up and down, eh?" Lucy nodded.

Prudence sat ahead of them in not quite the first pew. That was occupied by many middle-aged and elderly people. "Cricks," said Lucy, nodding toward them. The Cricks didn't seem to be paying much attention to Prudence, nor she to them, beyond a few nods as people came and went. There was a closed casket on the dais.

Gerry looked around and spotted Doug sitting with Andrew and Markie. She knew Blaise had an appointment that prevented him from attending. She saw Cathy arrive and slip in next to Andrew. Even Mary and Margaret were there, the one looking curious, the other pale and ill.

The priest and altar boys entered and the service began.

Gerry liked Father Lackey, having relied on him in a previous matter that winter. She smiled, wondering how his Jack Russell terrier Smitty was doing.

When the mass was over, Prudence slowly joined Gerry and Lucy. She'd been crying. "There, there," Lucy said and patted her arm. Gerry kissed Prudence's cheek and patted the other arm; words stuck in her throat.

When Prudence was ready, they went downstairs to the basement for refreshments. It was a simple wake: sandwiches and cookies, coffee and tea. Prudence's friends and relations clustered around her. Gerry thought, thank goodness it looks as if Mary and Margaret have left. Doug gave Gerry a kiss, then left her to comfort Prudence.

The Cricks kept to themselves, though people approached them from time to time to offer condolences. Gerry wondered if she ought to as well but decided she was there to support Prudence, not the relatives of a man they'd spurned twenty-five years ago.

She bit into a tuna sandwich and locked eyes with the elderly man who'd driven by her house in the white car. She turned away, hoping her eyes hadn't bulged in astonishment and asked Prudence who he was.

Prudence turned around to look. "Him? He's Alex's older brother, Jack. Why?"

Gerry told the truth, or part of it. "Oh, he was looking at cats last weekend when I did the CRAS adoption event."

Prudence looked surprised. "Him? I remember him laughing once when his tractor crushed a barnyard kitten. At the Crick farm. You say he was looking at cats!?"

Gerry dissembled as best she could. "Oh well, you know, people change. Or maybe it wasn't him. Never mind. Good sandwiches."

When she saw people beginning to leave, and after offering Prudence a lift, which was declined, and kissing all her friends, Gerry went. She did a little shopping in Lovering before going home. And before she made herself her afternoon coffee, she circled the outside of the house, checking for anything amiss. All was well. She noticed clumps of crocuses were still rising from the damp earth in different places in her garden. They must not all come up at the same time, she reasoned. There were some other blooms new to her that looked like very short individual irises. Fat hyacinth buds were forming. The little flowers soothed her. She went inside to her cats.

17

"All right. What's going on?"

Gerry had driven through the rain to Prudence's for 8:15 the next morning, as Prudence had said she wanted to do one long day's cleaning of The Maples. Prudence had driven them back to Gerry's house and parked. Gerry had made coffee and was just about to take that first warm soothing sip when Prudence appeared in the living room. "What was all that about Jack Crick yesterday? Come on. I know you. Tell me."

Gerry meekly asked her friend, "Coffee?"

Manners asserted themselves and Prudence said, "Please."

Gerry poured it for her. "We better make ourselves comfortable." They each took a rocking chair. There was no fire, but the cats, sensing drama, began to skulk into the room. "First of all, look at this." She handed Prudence June's latest. "She's done it again."

"Mother and Isabelle," Prudence said slowly. "And your kitten." Puzzled, she looked at Gerry. "How would June Conway know my mother was a twin when that twin died so many years ago? Jay, I get." They both looked at the kitten who was concentrating on a ladybug crawling up the wall just out of her reach. "I mean, June's been seeing Jay every week for a while now so that kind of makes sense."

"Yee-es. But about Isabelle. Look how thin June's made her." Gerry shuddered. "Almost — skeletal. Prudence, I don't think June is drawing from an old photograph she may have seen. I think she's drawing the dead."

There was a pause, filled by the patter of raindrops. "If so," Prudence began. "If so, why is there a living creature among them, the kitten, I mean?"

"Well, look. The girls are pointing at Jay like she's significant, the answer to a question we don't yet know." Jay was on her hind legs, stretching up the wall, trying to fly.

Gerry kept going. "They're on my back lawn. But they're your close relatives, as well as mine. So we're both involved, Prudence." She thought of Mrs. Smith, a medium both Prudence — regularly — and   Gerry — infrequently — consulted. "Prudence, what about a visit to Mrs. Smith? To ask about the people on the lawn."

"No." Prudence's reply was quiet but emphatic.

"No?"

"No." She fidgeted for a moment. "I'm afraid to."

"Afraid? But your mother — "

"It's not Mother I'm afraid of. I'm afraid, I'm afraid, Alex — " Prudence looked distressed.

"Ohhhh." This pause was awkward. "I understand." Gerry waited a few seconds. "Well, back in the real world, both our properties have been vandalized, and we've both received threatening messages — yours on a bit of paper and mine scrawled all over my house." She took a deep breath. "I think I know who sent them."

"Well? Who?"

"At first I thought it was Margaret but now I'm pretty sure it was Jack Crick. At least the second time." She frowned. "Though Margaret may have egged my house. She sure acted like she knew about it when she rammed the house."

Prudence was not to be distracted. "Jack Crick!? Are you kidding? You just met him yesterday!"

"Jack Crick watched me for most of last Saturday during the cat thing at the mall."

"You said he was looking for a cat!"

"I don't think he was serious. When I went to the bathroom, he followed me. I hid — not in the bathroom, but around the corner from it — and saw him walk by looking for me. I saw him drive by the house last Wednesday. And he didn't care that I saw him. He was driving a small white car. Isn't that what your neighbour said he saw leaving your house when it was broken into?"

"Jack Crick trashed my window boxes, broke my front door and left a message asking 'where is it?'? Why? And what's 'it'?"

By now the cats, fascinated by the energy between the women and probably relieved that Prudence's arrival had for once not signalled the release of the vacuum cleaner from its lair, were mostly all gathered in the living room. Rain dripped off the roof. Outside the warming earth gave off a vapour.

Gerry stood and began to pace. Jay followed her as she passed the hearth rug, where Mother, Ronald, and the boys were sitting. Their heads tracked her progress. "Let's break it down." She reached the end of the room, and paused, where more cats had arranged themselves in a row on the long bench under the windows. "First the messages. They tell me, they're watching, and you, they want something. So they think you know where it is and they think — " She looked out one of the front windows. "They think the thing is here!" Jay leapt on the windowsill and paraded back and forth.

"Well! Your mind does jump about!"

Gerry returned to stand on the hearth rug, Jay at her heels. The cats there looked up at Gerry. "Wait. Now, I know you think I don't take your, er, communication with your mother through Mrs. Smith seriously. But as I've gotten to know you, and because of things that have happened in the last year since Aunt Maggie died, I'm prepared to concede that there may, there *may* be emanations coming from the dead. And that some people, or cats, are more sensitive to these emanations than others are." The cats tried to look modest.

Both Gerry and Prudence looked toward the lake. Bob, lazing on Gerry's work table, seemed to know to what they were referring. He sat up, yawned terrifically and moved to sit looking out at the backyard.

"Exactly," Gerry said. Jay jumped up and sat with Bob, also looking out.

The women walked over to the window. "So you think," Prudence began slowly, "that our dead kin are assembled out there and are trying to communicate or warn us through a cat? What about, exactly?"

"I'm not sure but I think so. And June Conway is sensitive to, ah, the other side, and can't help but draw it."

"And Jack Crick? Come and sit down. I don't feel good staring out the window at that mist."

Gerry said, "I'm going to make a fire. It's a dreary day and it will make the room cozy."

"And I'm supposed to be working!" Prudence went around the house, whipping hairy towels off of upholstered surfaces and replacing them with clean ones. She set the washing machine going. They each took another cup of coffee and sat back down.

"Prudence, just tell me anything you remember about Jack Crick or any of Alex's other brothers. No, wait, wait." She got up and rummaged among her papers. She found Aunt Maggie's exercise book of little stories and handed it to Prudence. "Read this first."

It didn't take long for Prudence to read "The Bad Boy." It filled barely one page. She sighed and rested the book on her lap. "A very observant little girl, your aunt."

"Yes. Very. So I never knew this family and didn't live in that time, but I get that they were poor. I mean, lard in a sandwich? Rubber boots instead of shoes or warm winter boots? Twelve kids living with parents who can't read? It sounds bad."

"They were farmers. Alex was one of the younger kids. Jack was the oldest, a bit of a bully to the younger ones. He and a couple of the other brothers took on the farm when the father got too old. The mother died in her fifties." Prudence snorted. "Probably of exhaustion."

Gerry asked, "Anything more about Jack?"

"He was wild for a time. Went to prison for, I think it was, car theft. When he got out he seemed calmed down. Took to farming. Got drunk at our wedding and had a fight with the best man." She stopped talking abruptly.

"Bad memory?" Gerry asked sympathetically.

"Um. Yes." Bob let out a yowl. Both women jumped, then laughed, a bit nervously. "You weren't there, Bob," Prudence cautioned. "You don't know. Do you?" Bob lay on Gerry's cartoons and stared at Prudence.

"And that's it? He's a bully, went to prison and then farmed for the rest of his life?"

"That's it. I left Alex, or rather, I kicked him out of our apartment and didn't see or hear about the Cricks until the robbery.

"It was awful. The police didn't seem to believe me when I said Alex and I were separated. They searched my apartment. After that, I moved back in with Mother. My father had died a few years before so it made sense."

"At the cottage where you live now, Prudence?"

"Yes." Prudence spoke with irritation and exhaustion in her voice. "What good is raking up all this history going to do, Gerry?"

Bob yowled again. This time, neither woman laughed. Gerry felt abashed and kept silent.

Prudence changed the subject. "What's happening about your Borduas? Are you going to get any insurance money?"

Gerry replied as though distracted. "Huh? Oh. That. Marion and Bertie seem to think it could only be the big man himself who could get away with six art thefts in as many years. He seems to have motive. He needs money." She snapped to attention. "Prudence! That's it! It's about the money! Why Alex was killed! And why his brother Jack is haunting us! For the bank's money!"

"You think Jack needs money?"

"Maybe. Who doesn't? But more than that. I think — I think Jack was on the job with Alex and the others. Who knows? You say he was a bully. Maybe he was the one who smashed the bank guard's head. Maybe he threatened Alex to keep quiet. Wasn't Alex the only one who was caught?" Prudence nodded. "The scapegoat. The...the fall guy. Prudence, what if they didn't split the money and separate? What if Alex had all of it, hid it and didn't tell even the other robbers where? Cathy told me Alex wasn't caught for weeks after the robbery."

"Been gossiping?" Prudence's face was stony and her voice grim.

Gerry stammered. "Not, not really. I was just so shocked when you took me to visit him. I knew nothing about him and then met him in prison. I mentioned it to Cathy and she — "

"Never mind." Prudence's voice had reverted to its former weariness. "It's a mess. My life has been a mess. I'm going to clean the house." She stood up.

"But Prudence, what are we going to do about Jack Crick?"

"All we have is Jack in a white car driving past your house. That's it. Do you even know the make of the car?" Gerry shook her head. "So, is it worth mentioning to the police? Possibly. Will they take it seriously? I doubt it." She went into the kitchen for her purse and handed Gerry a card. "Here. This is one of the officers who talked to me after Alex's death. Call him if you like. I'm going to vacuum."

As the machine roared, the cats and Gerry melted away like the last drifts of snow in the rain.

"Hello. Coneybear. Here with four cats." Gerry had left the house without saying goodbye to Prudence. It had seemed like the best plan but now she felt bad. She leaned over the counter and lowered her voice. "Is Dr. Morin in?"

"Yes. That's who you'll be seeing. Which four cats?" Gerry didn't recognize this receptionist and grinned as the girl looked perplexedly from her computer screen to Gerry's face.

She laughed. "Today we have Cocoon and Max in here." She picked up one box. "And Bob and Ronald in here." She held up the other. "Is Dr. Perry in today?"

"Why? Would you prefer to see him? He's not in today but I could give you an appointment."

"No, no. That's all right. I'll just leave these guys here. I have to get something else from my car."

A half hour later and she was exhibiting the painting of Merlin to Dr. Morin. "That's lovely, Miss Coneybear. I'll give you a personal cheque. Now, let's look at some cats."

Max, a fluffy orange and white male, was first. "Hmm. Ten. He's in nice shape. Just brush him more often." Dr. Morin indicated a couple of mats of fur.

Gerry leaned in. "Oh dear. I hadn't noticed."

"The longhairs really need a weekly thorough grooming," the vet advised. "Or they clump." She vaccinated Max, and Gerry took out Cocoon, a fluffy grey and white female. Dr. Morin ran her hands across Cocoon's belly. "Like this," she said, exhibiting more clumps.

Gerry flushed. "I feel bad. I don't have time, obviously, and I've been neglecting them."

"I understand. You work. Your aunt didn't. I suggest you designate one day per week to groom all the cats." The normally reserved vet's eyes twinkled as she saw Gerry's face. "It won't take all day. Keep a list, if you like, and check them off as you do them."

This appealed to Gerry's task-oriented mind and she nodded. "These two are shorthairs, so I guess they're okay." She removed Bob first. He immediately lounged on the examining table.

"Hello, big guy," said the vet. "Nice. Next?"

Ronald squirmed out of Gerry's arms and disappeared behind the electronic scales. "He's a bit shy," she said, removing him. "Now Ronald, there's nothing to be afraid of."

The vet stroked him and exhibited a handful of hair to Gerry. "Some cats don't groom or don't groom well. You have to brush even the shorthaired ones or they'll suffer from hairballs."

"I will," Gerry promised, envisioning the cats lined up like soldiers while she sat at a desk with an array of combs, brushes, scissors and nail clippers in front of her, roll calling.

Everybody vaccinated, she paid with her credit card and tucked Dr. Morin's cheque in her wallet. On the way home she stopped at the bank and deposited the cheque. Then, thinking of a way to cheer Prudence, she purchased two almond paste dessert croissants at Lovering's bakery.

At home the vacuum could be heard droning away upstairs. Prudence had indicated she'd be putting in a long day to make up for the missed ones of the last few weeks. Gerry made her lunch and settled down to work.

Around three, Prudence made an appearance. "I'm sorry — "

At the same time, Gerry said, "It was wrong — "

They both stopped. "You go first," Gerry urged.

"No, you," Prudence said shyly.

"All right. I was wrong to discuss Alex with Cathy. I'm very sorry. It won't happen again."

Prudence blinked. "Thank you. I've already been talked about in this town so much — I'm sorry I got in a snit."

"You didn't really get in a snit. What a great word — 'snit.'" Prudence smiled. "You just kind of shut down. Which is understandable. I'm in the mood for tea. What about a pot of Earl Grey?"

"I'll make it," Prudence said. "I made scones last night — I know, I know — why was I baking when we'd just buried my husband? Why do you work all hours when things get difficult? Anyway, I've got some of them in my purse." She rattled around in the kitchen while Gerry tidied the table. Prudence returned with a tray of good things.

"Chocolate chip scones?" Gerry asked. "Gosh, I haven't had those since — " She thought back. "Since I stayed at Cathy's B&B when I came for Aunt Maggie's funeral. Imagine that. Almost a year."

"One year May 27th," Prudence said quietly.

Now that peace had been declared, several of the cats wended their way back into the room. That it was nearing their suppertime may also have had something to do with it.

The women sipped their fragrant tea and ate their scones. "Oh! I forgot! I bought those good almond croissants from the Lovering bakery. You know? The ones you like. Well," she admitted, "I like them too."

"What the hell," said her friend, "let's make this a real high tea. Bring them out." After licking her fingers, Gerry made up the fire. "Let's sit in the rockers," suggested Prudence. "I have more to tell you. And it's complicated."

Gerry wondered what was coming.

"Remember I told you Jack Crick got into a fight with the best man at Alex's and my wedding?" Gerry nodded. Bob jumped into her lap and sat like a sphinx, paws and face pointed at Prudence.

"Alex's best man was your father," Prudence said slowly.

"Dad? He never mentioned it. But, come to think of it, he didn't talk much about his life in Lovering, his later adult life, that is. I think he left under bad circumstances, or that was the feeling I got. But later he liked coming back here for visits." She added uncertainly, "I think."

"You must have wondered why he didn't inherit anything when his parents died."

"I wasn't born, Prudence! How could I wonder? And when we visited Aunt Maggie here I just assumed Dad was happy living in Toronto and Maggie was happy living in the family home in Lovering."

"I forget you're so much younger than me," Prudence murmured.

"I *feel* like I've aged since I moved here. Don't tell me I *look* it!"

"No. Of course not. You're a beautiful girl. Where was I? Oh, yes. The wedding.

"Remember when Markie first came back to visit Cathy and I told you I'd had a teenaged crush on her when she was a he?" Gerry nodded. "Well, like most teenagers, I had more than one crush. I liked my best friend's older brother too."

"Dad?" Gerry asked faintly.

Prudence nodded. "He was way too old for me. Ten years older." Gerry looked unhappy. "Oh, it's all right for you and Doug," Prudence assured her. "But it wouldn't have been right for a little teenager and a man in his twenties in the 1960s. No, I suffered in silence. Maggie probably knew but I doubt Gerry did."

"Gerry," the present-day Gerry repeated.

"That's what everyone called him," Prudence replied. "Anyway, I fell in love with Alex and we got married." She hesitated. "You may not know this, Gerry. Why would you? Your father was a bit wild himself, back in the day, and he and Alex, well, sometimes they ran with the same crowd. Maybe Jack Crick thought Gerry was leading Alex astray, him being so much older." Her tone grew bitter. "But I assure you Alex was the leader, if it was to do with any crimes."

"Crimes?" Gerry sounded incredulous. "My dad committed crimes?"

"Oh, you know: joyriding, drunkenness. But then Alex started dealing drugs, and I think that's when your dad straightened up. And began to pull away from Alex. But they were still friends, and when we got married Alex asked Gerry to be his best man."

Gerry digested all this. By now Bob was curled in her lap. Jay was similarly reposing on Prudence. "So that's what Alex meant when he called my dad 'The one that got away.' When we visited him in prison."

"I don't remember that. I was too wrought up. Maybe he meant the one who escaped Lovering before he got caught. Or was led into more serious crimes."

"Like bank robbery," Gerry said softly. "Or maybe Grampa Matthew sent him away. Because he was disappointed in him."

"Or to keep him safe," Prudence suggested. "Gerry didn't come home again until both his parents were dead, he'd married your mother and you'd been born. That's how I remember it." She rose and placed Jay on the hearth rug. "Now, let's feed these cats."

Thankful not to have to think about supper, Gerry drove to Bea and Cece's small townhouse in central Lovering. Bea had spaghetti with meatballs and salad all ready. As she sat down at their kitchen table with a glass of red wine, Gerry sighed and said, "I'm ready to make my will." Then, to her horror, she felt tears trickle down her cheeks.

"Now, now," said Cece awkwardly. "It's the Crick funeral. Not that you shouldn't make your will. But supper first, then we'll talk."

So, after the cookie dough ice cream and coffee, and after Bea had made herself scarce, parked in front of the television set with Cecilia, sister to Jay, on her lap, they did.

18

Gerry vowed to have a quiet Saturday. For once. She phoned Jean of CRAS and excused herself. "I'm neglecting the twenty I already have," she explained. "I'll try to come next week."

She drove to Lovering to purchase some heat-and-serve suppers. "Who am I kidding?" she muttered as she selected them from the store freezer. "I'd rather work and earn the money for convenience food than have to face cooking supper every night."

Two teenagers walked by, busy texting. They noticed her talking to herself and giggled. "That's right," she said in a slightly louder voice, "the crazy cat lady talks to herself in public," and walked straight into her Aunt Mary.

Well, their bodies didn't touch, but Gerry's cart gave Mary's a good whack. Margaret, who was steering the cart, hardly seemed to notice.

"Watch where you're going!" Mary snapped. She looked tired.

"Sorry," Gerry muttered. What are the odds I'd meet them again? she thought. She looked at her cousin uneasily. Margaret's eyelids drooped and she was humming tunelessly. Gerry looked back at her aunt. Was that a frown of concern disfiguring Mary's usually self-satisfied face? Gerry hoped she had her daughter on a tight leash.

She was done shopping so backed toward a checkout. She grabbed a fat Saturday paper and a bag of M&M's and got out of there. Once home, she popped a frozen lasagna in the oven and sat down with the paper. God damn it! She was going to relax! The phone rang. She decided to let it. It switched to her recorded message.

"You have reached the Coneybears at The Maples. Please leave us a message."

"Gerry, it's Cathy. Have you seen the paper? Call me!"

Gerry looked at the one she was holding, then reluctantly got up to speak to Cathy. "I'm here. I was just screening my calls. What's up?"

"Look on page ten. Have you got the paper?"

"Yes, yes. I just got home." She flipped through the paper. "Cathy, on page ten there's an article about how bad snow removal was in Montreal this winter and how much repairing all the potholes is going to cost."

There was a baffled silence at the other end. "Which paper are you looking at? I mean the *Lovering Herald*. Page ten."

"Hang on. I think I have it somewhere." Gerry rooted on the mantel above the fireplace among the envelopes and flyers that were the week's post. "I haven't had time to breathe this week, Cathy. Ah. Here it is." She sat back down and turned to page ten.

Heiress Will Work for Kibble was the headline. The byline read "by Judith Parsley." Gerry's eyes bulged. "Cathy, I'll call you back. Or not. Bye." She read on.

Local artist Geraldine Coneybear, who inherited Maggie Coneybear's prime waterfront property last year, isn't sitting as pretty as maybe she or others might have expected.

"Do you have any idea how much the annual maintenance of a house like The Maples is?" she told us. "And the cost of feeding twenty cats? And the vet bills?"

Coneybear, 26, a short vivacious redhead who drives a late model red and white Austin Mini Cooper, has been reduced to sitting in local malls trying to sell copies of her book *The Cat-Jumping Cakes of Dibble*.

"What?" Gerry roared, startling the cats who were sharing the living room with her. "Judith never wrote this!" Her eyes flicked back to the byline and she phoned the *Herald*. A recorded message. She hung up in frustration.

"Good grief! If I thought people were snickering about me before..." She read more of the article.

> According to her late aunt's will, Coneybear must live in the house and maintain the cats for five years, after which she may dispose of the property, and, we presume, the cats.

"You presume too much!" snarled Gerry. "As if I'd 'dispose' of you guys!" The cats looked gratified as she continued to read.

> Creator of *Mug the Bug*, a comic strip that runs daily in some of our competitors' papers, [Huh, you wish you had *Mug*, thought Gerry] and available to paint your house, spouse, child or dog (or even, dare we say, your cat!), Coneybear is an advertisement for how difficult, nay, [Nay? thought Gerry] even how precarious being a freelance artist can be.
> In these days of financial insecurity...

Here the writer went off on a personal rant about the future and how it might affect young people who didn't train for a specialized career, preferably in science or technology, before finishing with "So we wish young Gerry the best of luck in all her endeavours as she tries to fulfill her aunt's wishes."

"Too weird. I smell a rat," she told the cats. They looked as if they smelled one too, or would like to. "A Parsley-flavoured rat. But I like that the author mentioned I do freelance work. No bad publicity, they say?" The oven timer pinged and she brought her lasagna to the table. She was poised to dig in when again the phone rang. "Argh!" Again, she let it ring and go to her machine.

She managed two mouthfuls of lunch before Judith Parsley's teary voice began. "Gerry. I just phoned to apologize — "

Gerry jumped up and interrupted her. "I'm here, Judith."

"Oh, good. I didn't write it, Gerry. I'm so sorry. My father — I may have mentioned some things about you — you know, like, at the supper table." She gulped. "But he got it all wrong. I know you're not desperate, but, but hopeful and cheerful."

"I had a feeling it wasn't you, Judith. Once a newspaperman, always a newspaperman, I guess. Tell your father — you know what? I think a dignified silence from me is better."

Judith calmed somewhat. "All that stuff about not going into the arts but into science or technology — that was aimed at me!"

Gerry grinned to herself. "Yeah, I kind of got that."

"And he put my name on it to encourage me to follow in his footsteps, or something," Judith concluded.

"Yeah, I got that too. Anyway, I'm fine now. See you Wednesday."

Huh, she thought, returning to her lunch. Bill Parsley. Worried about his daughter. Probably regrets encouraging her to sign up for drawing lessons.

She finished her lasagna while reading the comics and her horoscope in the Montreal paper. "A good day to begin new projects but only if old ones are completed." She groaned. "I already have too many things going on." She moved to a rocking chair with the news section. For the second time that day, she did a double take.

TOP AUCTIONEER SOLVES MYSTERIOUS ART DISAPPEARANCES
EXCLUSIVE TO THE *TRIBUNE*.

Respected auction house Frey's of Montreal has revealed
that due to employee error six paintings were mislabelled
and languished in their storage facility for several years.
August Frey, owner-operator of Frey's, assured us the
problem has been rectified.

She phoned Bertie. "Smith's Antique Furniture and Objets
d'Arts," he answered smoothly.

"What's been happening!?" she exclaimed. "I've just seen
the paper!"

"Can't talk now. I'm between a possible armoire and a definite
silver tea set. Call you soon." He hung up.

Gerry exhaled in frustration. He was busy with clients.
She didn't have Marion's number. In exasperation, she flung
the rest of the paper aside and went to get her basket of cat-
grooming tools.

"Today's the day, cats," she announced. "Get ready." As by this
point only Jay and Bob were in the room, the announcement was
met with little attention. "I'll start with you two. Shorthairs. Hm.
Soft brush, I guess."

Bob reacted with pleasure and let her rub him all over. His
nails didn't seem too bad so she let them go. Jay reacted with joy,
seeing grooming as just another game to be played. Her nails were
overlong and one was split, but when Gerry tried to clip them,
the kitten ran away. "Possibly a two-person job," Gerry murmured
and wondered what Doug was doing.

She took the basket and moved through the house, gently
brushing while soothing her cats. Some of the longhairs let her cut
away mats, some didn't. She even managed to brush Lightning's

tortoiseshell-patterned head before the cat leapt sideways off the dining room table and out of the room.

After she was satisfied she'd at least tried to groom everybody, she ran herself a bath and read part of *Cider with Rosie* by Laurie Lee. The rural childhood poverty described by the author made her think of Alexander and Jack Crick and all their brothers and sisters.

She put down the book and closed her eyes. So tired. So... When she woke up the water was tepid and she was cold.

Downstairs, she made a fire and a coffee and poured the M&M's into a bowl. The bath had been relaxing. She wondered if Bertie Smith would call her back. What had those two been up to? And without her!

The doorbell rang. She cringed. Oh, not on her day off! She looked for a car in front of the house. Nothing. So one of her neighbours. She walked to the front door. Andrew's worried face could be seen through the curtained window on one side of the entranceway. She let him in.

They hadn't met since Margaret had rammed Gerry's house. They embraced awkwardly. "Coffee?" He nodded and they went through.

"Ah, a fire. What a good idea." He folded his length into a rocker and extended his legs. "What a week!"

"Tell me about it!" she agreed from the kitchen. "Where's Markie?"

"Oh, she went home a few days ago. Thanks." He took the steaming libation and sipped gratefully. Gerry offered the bowl of candy and they munched for a few seconds. "She's the one good thing." He smiled. "She put her house on the market."

"Andrew! Does that mean — ?"

He nodded. "It's official. We're together. I introduced her — with much trepidation — to Mother and Margaret. It didn't go as badly as I feared. Mother's impressed by Markie's job."

"Is she still determined to sell Margaret's house out from under Doug and the boys?"

He grimaced. "I feel responsible for that. I told her it doesn't make sense she runs that big house just for herself. Anyway, she can't. I've been paying the bills for her at the bank. Her money's running out. Who knows when or even if the life insurance on Dad will pay out? She needs to downsize but instead she dreamt up this fantasy of Margaret and the boys living with her. What she's starting to realize is Margaret is only barely functional. I think Mother thought she was getting her little assistant back when she talked the doctors into releasing Margaret into her care." He sighed. "It's Margaret I want to talk to you about. I brought my chequebook."

Gerry went upstairs and got her household accounts. She handed the bill from the Hudsons and told him how much she'd paid Doug to help them repair the front of the house. He held his head. "God, what a mess. Gerry, what should I do?"

Gerry, who'd never had a sibling, was at a loss. "What's best for everyone?" she suggested softly. Privately, she thought it was time for Aunt Mary to grow up. "I think Aunt Mary is the key," she said. "Have you told her she's almost out of money?"

"I have."

"She must be frightened. Tell her you'll always be there in an emergency but you need your money for your new life with Markie."

"And Margaret?"

"There's no reason Aunt Mary can't find a two-bedroom apartment and share it with Margaret. But expecting the boys to move in to help look after their mother — you must see that's to be avoided? Andrew?"

He sighed. "Yes. Of course. We must put the boys first. Obviously Doug is the best person to look after them."

"Obviously." She hesitated. "And, Andrew. You know Margaret needs more help? She doesn't look at all well."

"I know. I'll arrange a meeting with her doctor." He sighed. "So we've sorted everybody out then," he said, rising to his feet. "If only they'll stay sorted."

Gerry stood on tiptoe to kiss him goodbye. "That's the trick," she said.

It hurt Gerry to see the "for sale" sign at the end of Doug's long driveway, but she hoped she had encouraging news to relay. Over the phone, he'd said the boys were out for the afternoon and evening. She fed the cats, not knowing when she'd return. When she arrived, Doug was raking his lawn and pulling mulch off the little garden.

He grinned at her. "Hello, lovely. What a great day, eh? I'm tidying for prospective buyers. Geoff's over at Mary's doing the same for her lawn and gardens. I was just about to take a break. What can I get you?"

"A coffee would be nice, Doug. No, on second thought, do you have any chips? Or nuts? I feel like something salty. I'm all sugared-out. I just had coffee and M&M's with Andrew. Guess what?" she asked as they went inside. Didi ran up the basement stairs to join them.

"What?"

"Andrew and Markie! They're going to live together!"

"That's kind of fast," Doug commented. "Didn't they just meet at Christmas?" He put out food for the cat.

Gerry counted on her fingers. "Okay, so four months is quick. But I think Andrew's been waiting so long, and maybe Markie, too, that they're just going for it. Doug? Doug! What is it?"

Doug was looking bleakly at her. "I've been waiting a long time too, Gerry."

She became aware of her heart — beating — beating. Was this going to be bad? Or good? She picked up Didi.

Doug gulped then continued. "I know we've only been together a short time, but I wanted to say, I want to say — "

"Hi, Dad! Hi, Gerry! What's for supper? Hi, Didi! Who's a bad girl? Trashing my homework." David chucked the kitten under the chin then stood in front of the open fridge. "Gosh, I'm hungry!"

Doug shrugged and smiled at Gerry. "To be continued," he said. Her heart calmed. It was good. It was going to be good. "I was just getting Gerry some pop and chips. That do you until we can heat up a pizza? What happened to your shift?"

"Great. Store was dead so I was the lucky bagboy who got sent home. After I fired all the expired meat and stuff down the chute into the trash compactor. Geez, it stinks. We call it the baby eater."

"Ew!" said Gerry, as David joined her at the kitchen table while Doug worked. David continued, "And I loaded up the beer fridge for Saturday night."

"Sounds like they keep you busy, when you are there," Gerry began. She switched gears. "I may have good news. I had a long talk with Andrew and he's going to try again to get Mary to sell her house and move to an apartment. So you guys may not have to move."

"And Mum?" David spoke uncertainly.

"We hope she can live with her mother." Gerry looked at Doug. "That would be better, wouldn't it? If you could just stay here?"

He gave her a cool look. "You'd like us to stay here?"

She felt stricken. "Oh — " She looked at David, who was flipping through the local paper. "I didn't mean — I would love — " She lowered her voice. "I was counting bedrooms at my house, if you must know. In case — "

His aspect changed, warmed. "Were you?"

"Hey, Gerry, look at this! Judy wrote about you!"

Doug came over and quickly scanned the article.

Gerry quipped, "Yeah, I'm getting business cards printed up with my name and number on one side and 'Will work for kibble' on the other."

David snickered. Doug raised his eyebrows.

She shrugged. "I'm over it. And it was Judy's father who wrote it. Who knows? It may raise my profile locally. I may even get some business out of it."

The bag of chips was finished. David ate half the pizza while Gerry and Doug split the other half. David took a bag of cookies, a large glass of milk and the cat into the TV room off the kitchen.

Doug reached for Gerry's hand. "I don't want us to rush. And I am touched that you even considered for a moment taking in me and my three boys."

"I must confess I did feel nervous about surrendering that much of my space," she admitted, twining her fingers with his. "But I was looking forward to having a resident handyman."

"Oh, were you?" He kissed her. "Come on. I want to show you more of my neon designs. In my room."

"Really. Neon designs. How interesting." They laughed softly as they went upstairs.

19

Gerry woke, confused. The phone was ringing. But she didn't have a phone in her bedroom. She opened her eyes and heard Doug's voice. "Geoff? What — ?" He paused, listening. "Did you call the police? Okay, okay. I'll do it. Are you safe? Okay. Stay there, you hear me? Don't open the door until I or the police get there." He hung up the phone. "Jesus Christ," he said in a quiet voice. He took a breath and punched in three numbers. "Come on, come on."

"Doug, what is it?" Gerry started to dress. It was dark outside. She still felt disoriented.

He held up a hand as he spoke into the phone. "My son just called me about an accident at his grandmother's house." He gave Mary's address, then his own. "My ex-wife is also there and she is violent. My son has locked himself in an upstairs bathroom. All right. All right." He hung up. He'd managed to dress while talking.

"Gerry. Drive me to Mary's house." They ran downstairs. "David!?" Doug yelled. The boy's startled face appeared in the doorway of the TV room. Doug spoke clearly. "I'm going to pick up Geoff." He hesitated. "If your mother comes by, don't — you know what? Come with us."

They piled into the Mini and Gerry began slowly negotiating the deeply rutted rock and sand driveway. She saw the time. 9:15.

"Geoff's okay. He says — I'm sorry, David — he says Margaret took a knife to Mary. He ran to a bathroom and locked the door. I don't know what we'll find." He was patting his pockets frantically, looking for a cigarette. He didn't find any. "Damn it!"

David and Gerry were silent. Gerry felt tears coming into her eyes and brushed them away. David spoke in a strangled voice. "Dad — Mum — "

"I'm sorry, David. She's sicker than we thought."

Gerry couldn't help noticing that no one had a thought or concern for Mary.

"I think you two should stay in the car when we arrive," Doug began. "And lock the doors."

God, I hope the police get there first, Gerry prayed silently.

They pulled into Mary's house's large driveway. First on the scene. Gerry cut the engine and they listened. Mary's car must be still at the garage. A strange car with rental plates was parked in the driveway. There were a few lights on in the house, including one on the second storey. "Is that the upstairs bathroom, David?" Doug asked.

"One of them."

Doug cursed. He opened his door. "I have to go in."

Gerry got out too. "Doug, two is better than one. In a fight."

David also got out of the car. "I'm not staying here alone."

Doug cursed again, this time more extravagantly. "All right, but for chrissakes, stay behind me." They advanced up the central path to the front door. Doug took a breath and pressed down on the handle. The door opened a crack. "Oh, shit," he breathed.

He eased the door partway open then flung it wide. Nothing stirred inside. "Where are the fucking police?" he asked.

Gerry tugged at his arm. "Mary may be bleeding. We have to find her." He nodded and they moved through the hallway towards the kitchen where a light gleamed.

"Mum?" David said in a quavering voice. Nothing stirred. They entered the kitchen.

Amidst the chaos of counters swept clean, drawers half open and debris on the floor, they saw the remains of a meal for three on the table.

"So Geoff stayed for supper," Gerry said. "And then — " A sound from upstairs made them all jump. They heard a thump, then Geoff's voice called faintly.

Doug forgot caution and quickly returned to the hallway, taking the stairs to the second floor two at a time. David's long legs carried him close behind his father. Gerry followed.

"This way," David said and led them to a door with a thin strip of light underneath.

"Geoff?" Doug asked cautiously.

The tearful voice of his second son replied, "Dad?" The door opened. "Dad!" He fell into his father's arms. They all crowded into the bathroom and Gerry locked the door. There was blood on Geoff's pants.

Doug held him at arm's length, examining him. "Are you hurt? Did she cut you?"

Geoff shook his head.

"Mary's blood?" Gerry asked.

The boy nodded, then began to shake. Doug held him close. "It's all right. It's all right." Then he asked, "Where, Geoff? Where did it happen?"

The boy gulped and fought for control. "It...it started downstairs at supper. Gramma was talking, talking — she'd been drinking wine — telling Mum she just had to make more of an effort, and Mum went crazy, wrecking the place, and when Gramma tried to stop her, she grabbed a knife and — "

"Mary's not in the kitchen, Geoff," Gerry said urgently.

"She, she ran upstairs, to her room, and Mum followed her. I went up too. I didn't see the attack but I...I tried to stop the bleeding. But Mum — " Here he paused and looked, bewildered, at his father. "Mum screamed at me, Dad, to leave Gramma alone, and I got scared so I ran in here."

Doug patted him. "Good boy. Good boy. You did right. Oh, thank God." They'd all heard the sound of approaching sirens. Doug flung open the bathroom window as the police and emergency vehicles screeched into the driveway. "Up here," he called. "I'm the one who phoned for help. I'm locked in with my sons and my girlfriend. We think my ex-wife is somewhere in the house, possibly with a knife." He paused and whispered, "Jesus, I can't believe what I'm saying." He raised his voice again. "My mother-in-law is upstairs in another room, wounded." He drew himself back into the room. "That's it, guys. Now we wait."

"And she was singing?" Prudence's voice sounded incredulous.

"Not singing so much as humming. Humming and rocking. And every now and then she put out a hand and touched Mary. And she was still holding the knife!" Gerry shuddered as she recalled her, Doug, Geoff and David crowding behind the cops as they tried to get Margaret to drop the knife. And their relief when they saw Mary was still breathing. "It was awful for the boys. Doug went with the police and Margaret, I called Andrew so he could go to the hospital for his mother, and I took Geoff and David home. To their home. We had some food there, they called James who got a friend to drive him home from Montreal. We all slept for a bit, then I came home to feed the cats." Tears welled up. "David didn't want me to leave. He was shaking. So I went back over there to wait for Doug to get home. Then I came home and crashed."

She looked around her with affection. The sun shone into the living room, the coffee in her mug tasted good, her best friend and her twenty other best friends were there to comfort her.

Prudence leaned over and quietly said, "It's brought you all closer, hasn't it?"

"To Doug? Definitely. And to the boys. Geoff and David, anyway. Two down, one to go. James is still a bit remote."

"Have you heard from Andrew? About Mary?"

"She'll recover," Gerry said grimly, "and live to make her relatives' lives miserable again, no doubt."

Prudence stood up. "I want to wash all the floors today and both bathrooms, so I'd better get cracking."

"And I," muttered Gerry, "have a visit to make." She looked up a name and address in the phone book, then left Prudence to her chores and drove along the river road towards Mrs. Smith's. If Prudence wouldn't do it, she, Gerry, would.

I'm going to consult a medium, she said to herself, as she took the elevator to Mrs. Smith's modern apartment. I'm actually going to consult a medium. For the second time in my life.

Once seated with closed eyes at Mrs. Smith's glass and metal table, Gerry let her doubts go. She trusted Prudence who trusted Mrs. Smith. Therefore, she, Gerry, must trust Mrs. Smith.

"You know I can't call up any specific spirit?" Mrs. Smith asked in her gentle voice.

Gerry opened her eyes. "Yes. I know. But if you could ask if anyone has news of Alexander Crick? He just passed. Maybe his spirit is close?"

Mrs. Smith smiled. "It's hard to describe what we're doing in words but I think I see what you're trying to do." They both closed their eyes and waited. After what seemed like ages to Gerry, Mrs. Smith asked, "Is there anyone there? Does anyone want to contact Miss Coneybear?"

Gerry felt her neck hairs move. "Yes?" asked Mrs. Smith politely. I wonder what her first name is, Gerry thought.

"Yes?" repeated the medium. Then, "It's your father."

Gerry felt an electric shock at the tips of her fingers. She whispered, "Dad?"

"Alex is with him, he says. Alex doesn't want all that — " Mrs. Smith paused. "All that sacrifice to go to waste."

"Sacrifice? What sacrifice?"

"Alex says he did it for his mother. One son, not two. One son, not three."

But Gerry was distracted. "Is my father all right? Is he — happy?"

Mrs. Smith waited. "I'm not feeling any unhappiness. From either of them."

"But — "

"We can only wait and accept, Gerry. They rarely answer questions."

"Okay. Just try one. Ask Alex. What about Jack?"

Mrs. Smith waited. "I'm sorry. He doesn't want to talk about Jack. He just keeps saying 'sacrifice.'" She waited a bit longer. "They're gone, Gerry. I'm sorry if you're disappointed."

Gerry felt as though someone had punched her in the stomach. That her father was there. Close. But disengaged from her in a way she didn't understand. It hadn't been like the cozy chats she imagined Prudence having with her dead mother.

Mrs. Smith struggled to help her. "I think they don't mean to be unkind. It's just different. Where they are. Some are more reticent than others. I know this is a ridiculous thing to say, but don't take it personally."

Gerry gave her a weak smile. "Mrs. Smith, what's your first name?"

"Amélie," said Mrs. Smith. "Why?"

"I just wondered."

Gerry pulled over at the river side of the road and looked at the narrow two-storey farmhouse at the end of a long straight driveway. Isolated, the house stuck up into the air. She imagined it exposed to the winter winds, unprotected by any tree.

She considered whether she better leave this visit until someone, preferably someone larger than her, could accompany her. Then she remembered all the work and expense of removing the graffiti from her house, Prudence's shattered window boxes and door, Alex Crick's dead battered body, and Prudence's numb sorrow at his funeral. Bullies should be stood up to, she thought.

She decided to leave her car where it was and walk in. She knocked at the front door, waited, then walked to the back door. She cupped her eyes with her hands and peered into the kitchen. A stove, a fridge, an old rectangular table and two chairs. A calendar on one wall and a clock on another. She turned and looked at the blue pickup truck parked near one of the barns. No white compact car that she could see.

She walked to the first barn, stuck her head in and called, "Hello?"

An elderly man with a faint look of Alex Crick, looking older than Jack, came out of a small room, wiping his hands on a rag. He had on overalls like garage mechanics wear and rubber boots. "Who'r you?" he said. He had the palest blue eyes she'd ever seen.

"Gerry," she said. "I'm looking for Jack."

"Jack's out," he replied. He half turned away.

"In his white car?" she couldn't resist asking.

"We have a white car." He paused, waiting.

"And you're his brother?"

"I'm Robert," he said. One of his eyelids had a permanent droop.

"I didn't see you at Alex's funeral."

"Didn't go," was the terse reply. His eyes were expressionless.

"Okay, Robert, just tell Jack I dropped by."

"What's yer name again?"

"Gerry." She was beginning to think he was maybe a bit slow.

"You talk a lot," he said, his pale eyes dull, and he took a step toward her. She took a step back but he seemed to lose interest and turned away, back to his task, as though she really didn't matter at all. He gave her a peculiar feeling.

She got into her car with relief and, as she drove home, trying to calm herself, she wondered if Jack Crick would ever get her message. She needn't have worried. His car was parked in front of her house and he was sitting at her dining room table.

Prudence hadn't even made tea or coffee. After the emotion of the séance and the thinly veiled menace at the farm, Gerry needed one or the other, so, after taking in the tension in the dining room, she made a pot of tea and plunked it and three mugs on the table between them.

The usual cats sat in the usual chairs at the table. Gerry wondered if Jack Crick knew or cared he was being observed by so many pairs of feline eyes.

She sat at the head of the table and asked, "What's it all about?"

Prudence got in first. "Jack, here, has a proposition for us."

"Oh yes?" Gerry said cautiously.

"Seems he read about you needing money in the local paper." Gerry, surrounded by all the accumulated comfort of 200 years of Coneybear residence at The Maples, tried to look poor.

Crick himself spoke. "Alex always said he'd buried the money where no one would ever look. 'Somewhere fruitful,' was all he said."

"Wouldn't he have buried it somewhere on your farm?" Gerry asked.

"'Somewhere fruitful,' he said. That's never been our farm."

Prudence, never taking her eyes off the man, said, "Jack is proposing we share the money if we find it."

Gerry gave him an appraising look. "Now why would he do that, I wonder?"

Jack leaned forward and spoke eagerly. "I think he buried it here. In the garden. Where his friend Gerry Coneybear lived. And I think he told you, Prudence Catford, exactly where."

Bob jumped on the far end of the table, appraised the situation, curled up and fell asleep.

Gerry asked, "You need money, Jack? What's changed? You have the farm. Why now?"

"I'm seventy-five years old, dammit, and I'm tired, that's what! But farmers don't retire. Can't afford to. Don't want to sell the farm. Just want to retire on it. And Robert — "

"Robert wouldn't do well off the farm, eh, Jack?" Gerry said softly.

"How do you — ?"

"I was just there, looking for you."

Prudence twitched and gave Gerry a look, but continued the inquisition. "Robert was always your mother's 'special' boy, wasn't he, Jack?"

Gerry took over. "I'm guessing Robert wouldn't have survived prison, would he, Jack? So Alex took the rap."

Both Prudence and Jack turned to look at Gerry with surprise. Out of the corner of her eye she saw Jay enter the room, hesitate, then join Bob. "Alex sacrificed himself for you and Robert, didn't he, Jack? To save your mother the pain of three sons in prison instead of only one."

Jack looked stupefied. "How do you know — ?"

"And maybe it was Robert picked up the paperweight in the bank and smashed in the guard's head. Did the guard talk too much? Did he annoy your brother? And Alex? Was he slow about telling you and Robert where the money was or is hidden? After he got out? Or did he just annoy Robert too? So he beat him to death and left him in a ditch."

Jack stood up. "Look. I just want the money. Are you going to cooperate?"

Prudence and Gerry stood up as well. None of the cats in the room stirred. The two on the table watched. Prudence's voice was full of contempt. "What'll you do, Jack? Break some more of my house? Spray-paint Gerry's house again?"

He looked flustered. "That was just to soften you up a bit, make you —"

"You always were a bully and a mean bastard, Jack Crick." Prudence leaned in. "When I think Alex sacrificed himself for two like you and Robert, I'm sick to my stomach. Gerry, did you ever call that detective about seeing Jack drive by your house in his little white car?" Gerry shook her head. Prudence fixed Jack with her stare. "And my neighbour saw it too, after my place was trashed. Here's what's going to happen, Jack. Me and Gerry are going to write down what we think has happened: both twenty-five years ago and recently. Then we're going to seal it in an envelope, get it notarized and put it away in a safety deposit box to puzzle Gerry's great-grandchildren with a hundred years from now.

"That's if you're good. If there's any more nonsense about damaging our properties, or us, well, the envelope will get opened sooner rather than later, won't it? Now get back to your farm and keep an eye on your precious brother."

Jack Crick blinked a couple of times then left, slamming the door after him. They waited until they heard the sound of his car driving away before letting out a collective breath.

"Prudence, you were great! Weren't you scared?"

"Nah. Look at the cats. They hardly took any notice of him. He's not the one to be afraid of." She mused. "I bet he just tells Robert to work while he's away. And hopes for the best. Poor Alex."

Nervously, Gerry asked, "Are we just going to let them get away with it? Write it all down and put it away? Hope Robert doesn't hurt anyone else?" Like Uncle Geoff did with Margaret, she thought but didn't say. Like we did with Margaret.

"Hell, no. We're going to tell the police what we think. Let them question Robert. And Jack. Make them sweat a bit. More tea?"

20

"I wonder if anything will come of that?" Marion Stewart nodded in the direction of Bertie Smith and Prudence, who were taking their time exploring the garden and backyard of The Maples.

Gerry squinted from the screened back porch at the two, now by the shore. Bertie threw a rock at the lake. It sank with a plop. Prudence bent, selected her rock carefully and skipped it more times than Gerry could count before losing sight of it. The two down by the water laughed. "She's been through a lot," she said carefully.

"Bertie's a good sort," was Marion's concluding comment. "My, your daffodils look wonderful in the sun."

Gerry had to agree. What a difference a week had made! The weather had shifted to positively warm, the grass had dried out, and even the little blue flowers that each spring decorated local lawns, including hers, had come up, bloomed and faded. Perennials were emerging, mysterious clumps of green that would soon provide more colour in the garden. For now, it was the beginning of the month of bulbs: tulips, hyacinths, others Gerry was ignorant of, and the daffodils, her favourite.

Squirrels — black, grey and red — as well as chipmunks, chittered angrily at the human invasion of their garden. Squirrels, Gerry mused. Maybe her next animal painting would feature one or more of the little furry creatures. They were certainly a sign of spring, as were the workmen swarming the house next door, banging and shouting. Lovering was speeding towards summer and Gerry couldn't wait.

A whole load of worries now seemed light. She'd made her will. She was still unsure about parts of it but at least it was made.

Robert Crick had confessed to both murders. Jack Crick was going down as his accomplice. Apparently both brothers had long had reputations for violence and had already been suspects in their brother's murder before Gerry and Prudence told what they knew and suspected.

Gerry had decided it was time to produce Uncle Geoff's letter implicating Margaret in Aunt Maggie's murder. Margaret was under detention as it was decided if she was fit to stand trial for that crime (though as far as Gerry knew, there was still no evidence) and for the attempted murder of her mother (which, sadly, had been witnessed by Geoff Jr.). Gerry hoped Doug would eventually forgive her for not telling him how dangerous Margaret was. She thought he probably would.

Cats were using the cat flap like it was the entrance to a fast food restaurant, which for the hunters among them, it was. Many ginger, black, grey, white or varicoloured forms were dotted about the landscape, or lurking in the thickets and shrubberies. Seventeen had been to the vet. Only Blackie, Whitey and Runt remained to be doctored.

Gerry looked toward the house next door, where a tall woman with a black retriever on a leash conferred with one of the workmen. Perhaps she was the new owner. Perhaps they would become friends. Perhaps Gerry should now get quotes for all the work that needed to be done on The Maples. Surely, Frey's insurance would soon send her some money.

Marion and Bertie had taken the train that morning. Gerry had picked them up, and they'd gone for lunch at the Parsley Inn. Then she'd brought them home to tour The Maples and meet Prudence, who'd prepared a light tea of little sandwiches and scones.

Gerry refilled Marion's teacup, offered her clotted cream for her scone and asked, "So what did you two do?" So much had happened since she'd spoken to Bertie after reading the newspaper article about Frey and his shenanigans, and Bertie had left a message that he'd call back, that she'd decided to hear about the affair from the two sleuths in person.

Marion stirred sugar into her tea and watched Bertie looking up into a giant willow that trailed over the swimming pool. Prudence pointed up then down, and laughed. Bertie laughed too and looked at Gerry.

"One of the cats fell from the tree into the pool last summer," she explained. "I was swimming at the time."

Marion had at last arranged the right amount of jam, butter and cream on her scone and took a bite. "Ah," she sighed and leaned back. "You know, I love my apartment, the convenience of it, but a summer place. Yes, that might be something to consider."

"Marion, are you teasing me?"

"Not at all. There isn't much to tell. We asked for an appointment. Frey didn't have a clue what we were going to spring on him. We told him we knew he was the thief. We said we'd start rumours about Frey's in high society — that would be me — and among the dealers — Bertie's job — that would bring his company to its knees. Then we gave him a way out. And he took it. His chalet is up for sale and as soon as he's able, he's going to repay the difference (all very hush hush and unofficial, of course) in value to the owners of the paintings he worked the insurance fiddle on."

"How can we trust him? He might try to leave the country. And how will he square it with the insurance company?"

"I reminded him his adult children have to live in Montreal. They're all very well connected. He won't want to hurt their or his reputation. As for the insurance people, they're his problem. I imagine they won't rock the boat as long as he pays them back as well. And you know what?"

"What?"

"Your picture hadn't even been sold. It was still hanging in the chalet the day we all drove up there."

"If only we'd known! We could have stormed the place and caught him, er, red-hanging, as it were."

Marion shook her head. "Not even a pun. Bad, very bad. And, as I recall, you were the one who counselled prudence, not I." She washed the remaining delectable mouthful down with tea. "Anyway, don't feel sorry for Frey. I heard just yesterday he's hired his girlfriend to work at the business. Recycling money, indeed!"

Gerry laughed. "So where is it? My picture?"

"I believe," Marion said very slowly, "it's in Bertie's satchel. In your living room."

Gerry squeaked. From over under the apple tree decked in fragrant pink and white blossoms, Bertie was scraping in the dirt with his hands. He stood up and revealed a dirty black briefcase. Prudence called, "Gerry. One of the cats must have been digging. Come and see."

Kitten couldn't believe how much more fun the outside was than the inside of the house. She was the first one through the cat flap in the morning and the last one back in at nightfall. Even rain didn't bother her.

On this rainy evening, the girl had gone out and forgotten to secure the cat flap from the inside. None of the others were outside. Only Kitten.

She crouched under a shrub that had miraculously sprouted foliage seemingly overnight. Its broad round leaves protected her from the drizzle. Next to a large rock under the shrub seemed like the logical place to crouch.

Kitten was listening to little night sounds when she became aware of a thin mist seeping out from under the rock. A thin cold mist.

She blinked as the calico ghost took shape beside her. For once the calico didn't seem angry. It stretched and dug spectral claws into the earth. Then it bounded into the rain.

Kitten knew she was supposed to follow. Her skin quivered as little wet drops made contact with her short-haired coat. She followed the calico.

It stopped in the centre of the garden and sat down. Kitten stopped too, a few paces away. They waited.

From down by the swimming pool, Kitten heard childish laughter. She turned her head. There were the two little girls she'd seen once before. They were running towards the cats. They too stopped in the centre of the garden, then moved closer to the apple tree, playing a silly kind of game of giant steps. The calico followed them.

Finally they collapsed, giggling, on the lawn. One of them, the more substantial one, got on her hands and knees and pretended to *dig in the soil under the tree. The other one held herself and rocked with laughter.*

The calico watched all this with a superior look on her face, then stepped around the twins and began to dig. She made little impression.

Kitten ran over to help. As soon as she'd begun, the calico stopped its efforts and sat, watching. The twins crawled over and also watched.

Kitten dug and dug. The soil was cool and soft and wet. Not unpleasant. She dug until she touched something that was not earth, not rock. It felt something like the giant shiny container, the one with the tight lid, that the girl kept kibble in under the kitchen sink. Kitten had clawed at that often enough.

She dug until a corner of the container was visible. That was enough. It didn't smell of kibble. Too bad. When she sat back on her haunches and began to groom her front paws, the little girls and the calico cat had gone. The tree smelled fragrant. A breeze blew its petals on to the ground.

A rustle and a squeak made her freeze and crouch. With a leap she disappeared into the neighbour's hedge.

ABOUT THE AUTHOR

Born in Montreal and raised in Hudson, Quebec, Louise Carson studied music in Montreal and Toronto, played jazz piano and sang in the chorus of the Canadian Opera Company. Carson has published eleven books: *Rope*, a blend of poetry and prose; *Mermaid Road*, a lyrical novella; *A Clearing*, a collection of poetry; and *Executor*, a mystery set in China and Toronto; *In Which: Book One of The Chronicles of Deasil Widdy*, historical fiction set in eighteenth-century Scotland; book two, *Measured*; (book three — *Third Circle* — is scheduled for publication in 2021); and her Maples Mysteries Series: *The Cat Among Us*, *The Cat Vanishes*, *The Cat Between* and *The Cat Possessed*. Her second collection of poetry — *Dog Poems* — has just been published.

Her poems appear in literary magazines, chapbooks and anthologies from coast to coast, including *The Best Canadian Poetry 2013*. She's been short-listed three times in *FreeFall* magazine's annual contest, and won a Manitoba Magazine Award. Her novel *In Which* was shortlisted for a Quebec Writers' Federation award in 2019. She has presented her work in many public forums, including Hudson's Storyfest 2015, and in Montreal, Ottawa, Toronto, Saskatoon, Kingston and New York City.

Louise lives in St-Lazare, Quebec, where she writes, teaches music and gardens.

ABOUT THE BOOK

This book, *The Cat Possessed*, the fourth in the Gerry Coneybear series set at The Maples, was written in tiny increments because I acquired Jackie O., a four-month-old kitten, shortly after I began to write it.

Anyone who has been possessed by such a creature will know that like an active toddler, a kitten combines hours of trashing houseplants and paper, rugs and (and this is a new one for me) bathroom caulking, with hours of deepest sleep. As I have both many houseplants and many papers lying around (I don't much care about the rugs or caulking.), each morning, which is my time to write, became an exercise in frustration for both of us. Jackie wanted to play. I wanted to write.

My daughter named her and it is a coincidence that her name shares the same first letter as Jay, the kitten who is possessed in the book. And unlike Jay, who resembles her mother Ariel, she of the black body and white legs, who now lives next door with Graymalkin and Blaise Parminter, our Jackie is completely black.

Anyway, she is the new joy of our lives and gets along fine with our young husky Labrador cross Mata. (Mata had her moment of glory posing for Harriet the husky, one of the animal stars of book three — *The Cat Between*.)

So I will twitch a catnip mouse on a string with one hand while writing with the other. Today has proved no exception. And just as I'm ready to give up, the kitten conks out on my lap, fulfilling her prime role of author's cat.